Harlequin® Romance brings you

PATRICIA THAYER's

Home to Texas and straight to the altar!

A home. A family. A legacy of their own.

Mustang Valley has long been home to the
brotherhood. United by blood, trust and loyalty,
these men fight for what they believe in—for
family, for what's right and ultimately…for love.

Now it's time. Time for the next generation!

Brandon Randell is
The No. 1 Sheriff in Texas

Brandon pulled the truck up beside another one with the ranch logo printed on the door panel. He got out, opened the back door and helped Zach down from the raised vehicle. Before Nora found her way out the passenger side, Brandon was around the truck and helping her.

"Thank you," Nora said, feeling a shock from his closeness. It had been a long time since she'd felt a man's tender touch. Yet in the past week Brandon Randell's hands had become very familiar. Their eyes locked and she instantly felt more heat.

"At your service, ma'am," he said hoarsely.

PATRICIA THAYER

The No. 1 Sheriff in Texas

THE
TEXAS
BROTHERHOOD

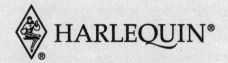

TORONTO • NEW YORK • LONDON
AMSTERDAM • PARIS • SYDNEY • HAMBURG
STOCKHOLM • ATHENS • TOKYO • MILAN • MADRID
PRAGUE • WARSAW • BUDAPEST • AUCKLAND

Recycling programs
for this product may
not exist in your area.

ISBN-13: 978-0-373-17655-7

THE NO. 1 SHERIFF IN TEXAS

First North American Publication 2010.

Copyright © 2010 by Patricia Wright.

For questions and comments about the quality of this book please contact us at Customer_eCare@Harlequin.ca.

www.eHarlequin.com

Printed in U.S.A.

Originally born and raised in Muncie, Indiana, **Patricia Thayer** is the second of eight children. She attended Ball State University, and soon afterwards headed West. Over the years she's made frequent visits back to the Midwest, trying to keep up with her growing family.

Patricia has called Orange County, California, home for many years. She not only enjoys the warm climate, but also the company and support of other published authors in the local writers' organization. For the past eighteen years she has had the unwavering support and encouragement of her critique group. It's a sisterhood like no other.

When not working on a story, you might find her traveling the United States and Europe, taking in the scenery and doing story research while thoroughly enjoying herself accompanied by Steve, her husband for over thirty-five years. Together they have three grown sons and four grandsons. As she calls them, her own true-life heroes. On rare days off from writing, you might catch her at Disneyland, spoiling those grandkids rotten! She also volunteers for the Grandparent Autism Network.

Patricia has written for over twenty years and has authored more than thirty-six books for Silhouette and Harlequin Books. She has been nominated for both a National Readers' Choice Award and a prestigious RITA® Award. Her book *Nothing Short of a Miracle* won an *RT Book Reviews* Reviewers' Choice award.

A long-time member of Romance Writers of America, she has served as president and held many other board positions for her local chapter in Orange County. She's a firm believer in giving back.

Check her Web site at www.patriciathayer.com for upcoming books.

To my readers.

For those of you who've been following
the Texas Brotherhood series since its conception
at Silhouette, and now to its new home
at Harlequin® Romance, here comes
the next generation of Randells.

CHAPTER ONE

BRANDON RANDELL sat in a booth at the coffee shop, toying with his mug. Anything to keep from looking across the table at his dad. Lately they hadn't even been able to share a meal without ending up on this same subject. The same argument. And Brandon couldn't tell him what he wanted to hear.

"I'm not sure I want to take over the running of the ranch."

"Well, son, when do you think you will know?"

Brandon hated being cornered about this…again. He met his father's piercing, dark gaze. Though in his mid-fifties, he looked much younger. Still big and intimidating, the years of physical labor had kept him in great shape. Some gray mixed in with his coal-black hair, and weathered lines around his eyes were the only differences he'd seen in the man in the past twenty-five years. That had been the day Cade Randell walked into his life and claimed him as his son.

Brandon leaned back in his seat, feeling the sudden weight of his sidearm, reminding him of his responsi-

bility to the people of Tom Green County, Texas. He'd
barely had a chance to stop for supper tonight.

He'd hoped the pressure to follow in the family's
ranching business had eased ten years ago when
Cousins Luke and Brady Randell returned to the valley
and helped form the Randell Corporation.

"I have commitments, Dad." He hesitated, then
rushed on to say, "This is my last week on patrol. I start
as a detective on Monday."

Cade blinked, then quickly covered his surprise.
"When did this happen?"

"I got the news this morning. I didn't want to tell you
and Mom about the promotion until I was sure it was a
done deal."

"Well, congratulations, son. We've always been
proud of your work with the sheriff's department."
There was a hint of a smile. "And your mother will be
happy you're off patrol."

"Thank you, Dad. That means a lot to me."

Again his father nodded. "All the more reason to
settle this situation. You have a commitment to the
family, too. Your grandfather willed the ranch to you,"
he stressed. "I've been running things along with your
brother, but you're past thirty, son. You should take it
over, or sell."

Hell, even more pressure. Well, he was the eldest.
The next generation of Randells. "Sell part of Mustang
Valley! Isn't there a law against that in this family?" he
tried to tease, but his dad didn't show any sign of humor.

"Joke all you want, but since your last birthday,

legally you own the land that the Randell Guest Ranch and the cattle operation grazing pastures are on. It's not fair to ask your brother to keep running things on his own. He's been working as the foreman. You need to make a decision, Brand."

Before Brandon could speak, his radio went off. "A possible 10-14 in progress," the dispatcher said over the radio. "Officer needed at the location of Burch and Maple, the West Hills Emergency Center parking lot."

Brandon reached for the radio and identified himself. "10-76 en route to West Hills Emergency Center. Arrival less than five minutes."

He slid out of the booth. "I've got to go." He was out the door and jogging to the patrol car before his dad could say anything.

Brandon shut everything else out of his head. It was all about his job now.

He had found her.

Nora Donnelly tried to draw a breath, but fear froze her. It wouldn't do her any good to fight, given the steely strength of the man who'd grabbed her and had her pressed against the car in the dimly lit parking lot. She was trapped.

"Thought you could get away with it, didn't you?" the attacker whispered harshly against her ear. "Well, I got you now."

"P…please, don't hurt me," she pleaded, thinking about her son. Oh, Zach. Who would take care of him? "Take whatever you want. I don't have much money on me, but I can get you some."

His hold tightened. "It's good hearing you beg. I don't want your money, but you are going to pay for what you did."

He swung her around. She faced the burly man, who towered over her own five-foot-five height. She didn't recognize him, but that didn't mean he wasn't sent here to find her.

Nora didn't have a chance to react before the man backhanded her across her face. The pain caught her off guard as she stumbled to the ground. He came after her as she tried to crawl away. He landed on top of her, trapping her against the asphalt. She screamed, trying desperately to fight him off. No, she wasn't going to be a victim again. She bucked and squirmed, until he grabbed one of her arms and twisted it behind her back. She cried out.

He straddled her from behind, knocking her head against the ground. She fought the pain and to keep conscious.

"Have I got your attention now?" he snarled.

"Please," she whispered, feeling his hands move over her. Bile rose in her throat.

Then came the distant sound of a siren. The attacker cursed. "I'm not done with you, yet." He climbed off of her and was gone.

Fighting the pain, Nora stumbled to her feet and searched around for her purse. She had to get away.

That was when she heard the siren cut off then footsteps. She glanced up at the large shadow. "Please, go away. Leave me alone."

"Ma'am, I'm Officer Randell with the sheriff's department." She saw his calming hand in the darkness as he brought his flashlight up to his shirt, showing her his badge.

Nora had always been good at holding it together. She had to, to protect her son. But suddenly her head began to pound and she closed her eyes against the pain. All she remembered was feeling the officer's arms coming around her and holding her close.

"Please… He can't find me again. Don't let him find me again."

"It's okay, you're safe now."

She wanted to believe his reassuring words, but knew no one could ever keep her safe.

Brandon shifted the woman's weight before she sank to the ground. He called for assistance and waited for help to come.

Don't let him find me again. He ran her words through his head as he brushed the woman's dark hair away from her face. Even in the shadowed light he could see she was young and pretty. Most abuse victims were, before some man got his hands on them. He should say fists.

Brandon took a breath to fight off memories of his early childhood, and the pain his mother suffered until finally she left her abuser, Joel Garson.

"You're safe," he assured her.

The woman groaned and turned her head toward his chest. A strange feeling came over him seeing the scrape along her jaw and the blood.

"You're going to be all right," he assured her again.

"Zach…" she whispered as tears flooded her eyes. "Oh, Zach, I'm sorry."

Had that been the guy who worked her over?

He heard footsteps and looked up to see people running toward them. "Over here," he called as he stood, lifting the small woman in his arms and carrying her to the gurney. He laid her down on the padded surface and started to step back when the woman opened her eyes. She gasped, and he could see the fear in her eyes and the tremble in her voice.

"Thank you," she managed to mumble as the nurse tugged a blanket over her to ward off the autumn chill.

Before Brandon could speak, a nurse stepped forward. "Nora," she whispered. "Oh, Nora, what happened?"

"Let's get her inside," someone else called.

Brandon would have followed the victim but another patrol car pulled up and rookie officer Jason Griggs emerged.

"We couldn't find anyone," the officer said.

"Did you secure the area?"

Together they walked back to the scene. "Yes, the security guards blocked off the exits and we're checking IDs. But we don't know who we're looking for." Griggs nodded toward the gurney being wheeled through the doors of the center. "Is the victim okay?"

"She was roughed up, but conscious." He found he wanted to see for himself. He shined his flashlight on the ground, then picked up an abandoned purse and found a wallet still inside along with the car keys.

Brandon opened her wallet and read her license. "This Nora Donnelly was lucky someone saw the man grab her."

Griggs joined in the ground search. "If the man wanted money, why didn't he just grab her purse and take off? He held her a lot longer than needed—unless he had other plans, like a sexual attack."

Brandon couldn't get the victim's words out of his head. Don't let him find me again, she'd begged him. Then she whispered the name "Zach." He glanced toward the emergency center. "I think I'll go see if Ms. Donnelly is up to answering some questions. Maybe give us a description."

Jason nodded as Brandon walked off. He had a strange feeling about this. When a man used a woman as a punching bag, it was more likely to be personal. Did Nora Donnelly know her attacker? Was Zach a husband or lover?

Once inside the sliding doors, he went to the large desk where a thin, middle-aged woman met him.

"Are you the deputy who saved Nora?"

He nodded. "I take it she works here?"

"Yes, she's a nurse," the receptionist said. "She'd just gotten off her shift…" The woman sighed with a worried look. "I knew that parking lot wasn't safe. They need to put in more lights."

"Wouldn't hurt. Has there been trouble before?"

The woman shook her head. "No, but you haven't caught this man, yet. He's still out there."

"Then make sure the security guard walks you out at

night. At least until we find this guy. Could you please tell me where they took Ms. Donnelly?"

"It's Mrs.—Nora's a widow and has the sweetest little boy." She smiled, then it slowly faded. "It's a shame she lost her husband so young."

So the attacker wasn't her husband. A boyfriend? Maybe. He shook his head. He had to stop speculating and talk to Nora Donnelly. "Where did they take her?"

"She's in exam room four. The doctor is with her now."

"Thank you," he told her.

"No, thank you…" She leaned in to read his badge. "Deputy Randell."

"Just glad I arrived in time." Brandon started off in that direction. His gut told him this was more than just an attempted robbery. This guy wanted to punish her, to hurt her.

Brandon stopped by the closed exam room door. He took a seat and waited, making notes about the incident and calling in to the station. It was another twenty minutes before a nurse came out. He stepped into the open doorway to see Nora Donnelly sitting up in bed. There was still a doctor and a nurse with her. When the doctor said something she gave him a teary smile, and Brandon couldn't seem to get enough air into his lungs.

In the light he could finally get a good look at her. She had a heart-shaped face with startling sapphire-blue eyes. Her nearly black hair hung to her shoulders in waves. His attention went to her mouth, full and inviting, especially the pouty bottom lip, giving him ideas he had no business thinking about right now. If ever.

She suddenly looked in his direction. He swallowed the dryness in his throat and managed to speak. "Mrs. Donnelly. Remember me, Deputy Randell?" He walked in, trying to exhibit authority as the nurse moved out of the way.

She tilted her head slightly. "Yes, Deputy, I remember you. You helped me. Thank you."

He shrugged. "It's my job. I believe this is yours." He handed her the oversize purse.

She hugged the bag close to her like a shield. "Oh, thank you."

Brandon found it hard not to stare at her. She was beautiful—even with her jaw bruised and bandaged. The only other imperfection on her skin was a faint scar along her eyebrow.

He finally managed to tear his gaze away and turned to the young doctor. "How is she?"

"She's doing fine, considering the slight concussion. She has some bumps and bruises, but I expect a full recovery."

"Then you don't mind if I ask her some questions?"

"Why don't you ask me if I mind?"

Nora Donnelly's soft, sultry voice lured his attention back to her. "I apologize, Mrs. Donnelly. Would you mind answering a few questions?"

When Dr. Jenson and Gloria tossed a wave as they left the room, Nora wanted to call them back. She didn't want to talk or think about the attack. It was her next move that was important. And what could possibly keep her and Zach safe.

She glanced up at the serious-looking deputy. He wasn't going to leave until he got answers.

"I'm not sure what I can tell you, Deputy."

"There are just a few questions." His gaze met hers. "Did you know your attacker?"

She hesitated, and knew he saw it right away. "No." It wasn't exactly a lie since she hadn't recognized him.

"Can you describe the man?"

"He was big, really big." She examined the deputy closely. No way she couldn't notice his dark good looks. Piercing brown eyes, coal-black hair and square jaw. "Much burlier than you." She shivered, recalling his body pressed against her.

"White, Hispanic, African-American?"

"White."

"Did he say anything?"

She flinched.

"Mrs. Donnelly." He stepped closer to the bed. "I know this is difficult but anything he said could be a possible clue to finding him."

Nora shut her eyes. She knew she couldn't lie—not about this. "He said, 'You thought you could get away with it.'"

She opened her eyes to find him watching her.

"You're widowed, correct?" the deputy asked.

She tensed, but managed to nod. "Two years."

He wrote in the notepad. "Could I get a list of your most recent male friends?"

"I can't give you one." When he started to press the issue, she stopped him. "There hasn't been anyone in my life since my husband. Only my son."

Brandon found that hard to believe. "Surely you've had men ask you out. Maybe someone who didn't want to take no for an answer? A coworker?"

She sat up straighter. "I'm a professional, Deputy. I don't date anyone I work with. I repeat, I don't date at all. Any free time I have I spend with my son."

Was she covering for some guy? "Who's Zach?"

She blinked in surprise. "Why do you ask?"

"You said his name when I found you."

"He's my son."

He nodded, checking him off the list. "What about someone who was once a patient here?"

Nora shrugged. "I think I'd remember a man that large." She took a breath. "Now, if you're finished with the questions, I'd like to go home."

Brandon hadn't meant to upset her. "Of course. I'll wait for you outside."

She paused. "I thought you were finished with the questions."

"I am for now. You have a concussion, so I'm going to be driving you home." He didn't give her a chance to protest, just went out into the hall.

Call it his detective skills kicking in a week early, but Brandon wanted more information from the pretty Nora Donnelly.

She wasn't telling him something. Something that could possibly help find her attacker. She may not have known him, but he had a feeling the man knew her.

* * *

Over an hour had passed before Mrs. Donnelly had been released and was ready to leave with Brandon. In the patrol car she'd been quiet, except when giving directions to her home. She let him know that she was done talking about the attack, so Brandon didn't even try asking her anything more.

So he took a different route. "How long have you lived in San Angelo?"

Nora kept her gaze on where they were going. "A few months." She paused, then said, "I wanted to make a fresh start for me and my son."

"Where are you from?"

She finally turned to him. "Phoenix, Arizona. Is there a reason for your interrogation?"

He shrugged. "I thought I was carrying on a conversation."

"Since my head is pounding, I'd appreciate it if we didn't exchange pleasantries right now."

He nodded. Ten minutes later, they drove through the security gate at her apartment complex. The place was newly built, less than two years ago. Brandon had thought about living here when he'd moved into town, but instead he'd bought a townhouse as an investment. Of course, he already owned a ranch with a big house that he could move in to anytime he wanted to go back.

Brandon turned down her street and Nora directed him to a parking space in front of her apartment. The car had barely stopped when she had the door open and was climbing out by the time he got to her side. She reminded him of the Randell women: independent and stubborn. He took her arm anyway.

Nora tried not to walk too fast, but she wanted to get inside and away from Deputy Randell. Not only did she long to get into bed and try to put this night out of her head, but she also couldn't let him delve any deeper into her past. If Jimmy sent this guy tonight, she had to think about her next move.

"Thank you, Deputy, for taking me home."

"Why don't I make sure you're safely inside?" He stepped closer, blocking some of the light. Nora drew a breath, inhaling his clean male scent. His gaze met hers, causing a strange warm rush down her spine. She quickly moved away, giving him room to work the key into the dead bolt, then allowing him to open the apartment door.

Nora walked into the small entry, set down her purse on the table, then went into the living area to find Millie seated in front of the television. Her son's babysitter turned around, then got up and rushed to her.

"Oh, Nora," she cried as she examined her friend's face. "You didn't tell me you were hurt this badly."

"Don't, Millie. Like I told you when I called, I'm fine. Really."

The gray-haired woman frowned. "You don't look fine. Remember, I'm a nurse, too." She glanced toward the deputy. "You must be Officer Randell. I'm Millie Carter, Nora's neighbor and babysitter for her son. Thank you for bringing her home."

"Not a problem."

Nora stepped in. "I have a slight concussion so I couldn't drive myself, but I'll need my car to get to work."

Brandon shook his head. "I don't think the hospital will be expecting you to work for a few days. But another deputy is bringing your car."

"Then you'll have time for coffee," Millie said before Nora could protest. "Cream or sugar?"

"Black, thank you," he said.

Nora wanted to call Millie back, but her strength was gone. She had to close her eyes, suddenly feeling shaky. The next thing she knew, the deputy reached out for her.

"Whoa." His arm came around her and he led her to the sofa. "You better sit down."

"I'm fine," she lied.

"You're not fine. It's probably a delayed reaction. Maybe you should go to bed."

"No!" She shook her head, trying to erase any thought of this man in her room.

He crouched down in front of her. "Nora, are you sure you're all right?" There was such concern in those dark eyes of his, but she couldn't let herself lean on anyone, especially a man. Never again. It wasn't safe for either of them.

"You've had a rough night."

All at once tears flooded her eyes. She tried to blink them away. "I'm okay," she lied. "I have to be."

Brandon couldn't stop the protective feelings he had for this woman. He wasn't supposed to get personally involved, but Nora Donnelly made it damn difficult.

"Such a tough guy?" he said with a smile. "Let

someone take care of you." He found himself reaching out and brushing a tear from her soft cheek. His voice softened. "You don't always have to be so strong."

"Yes, I do," she said.

Hearing the trembling in her voice, he pulled a blanket from the back of the sofa and wrapped it around her. "Are you cold?"

"A little."

He rubbed her arms, stirring up some warmth. She felt so delicate. He didn't want to think about what would have happened to her if he hadn't gotten there in time tonight. "Do you have any family I can call? Someone who can stay with you."

She looked at him with those startling blue eyes. His throat went dry and his chest tightened.

She finally shook her head. "Maybe Millie can stay."

"Mom?"

They both turned toward the hallway to find a small dark-haired boy in a pair of Star Wars pajamas. "Mom, what's wrong?"

Nora held out her hand as he walked toward her. "Zach, you shouldn't be out of bed."

"I heard you talking." The child's worried gaze took Brandon in, then searched his mother's face. "What happened?" His eyes showed fear. "Did he find you and hurt you?"

Brandon caught Nora's panic and knew his instincts were right. So maybe this attack wasn't one of random violence. But he didn't want the boy to worry.

"Hi, Zach, I'm Deputy Randell. Your mother had a

little accident in the parking lot at work, so I brought her home. She's okay now. I've made sure of that."

The boy looked at his mother. "You're really okay?"

She nodded. "I hit my head, so I have to rest for a few days." She studied her son. "Hey, I'm the one who's supposed to take care of you. How are you feeling tonight?"

"Okay."

She embraced the boy and Brandon could see the love between them.

"Then you should be back in bed, Zach," she told him. "It's late."

The boy pulled back from the embrace and shot Brandon a glance. There was worry etched on his face, far too much for a kid aged six, maybe seven.

"Your mother is okay, son," the deputy said. "The doctor checked her over."

That's when Millie came into the room, carrying a tray of mugs. "And I'll be here, Zach," she told him. "I'll take care of her like I take care of you."

Zach finally gave his mother a smile. "Okay." He kissed her then, and let Millie take him back to his bedroom. The older woman paused at the doorway. "Nora, yours is cocoa."

Brandon handed the mug to Nora, then took his. "He seems like a nice boy. He worries about you."

"There's no need." She stared down at her mug.

He took a sip of the hot brew. "Still it's got to be hard to raise a child on your own."

She stiffened. "I'm doing fine like a lot of single

mothers. Zach and I don't need anyone—we have each other."

"But what if you'd been seriously hurt tonight…or worse?" He had a hunch there was a lot more to this story. "The attacker worked you over good, Nora." He motioned to her face. "And what he said to you, 'You thought you could get away with it.'" He watched Nora's face…her jaw tensed. "Statistics show that personal attacks, like the one to your face, often mean the perpetrator is familiar with his victim."

"For the last time, Deputy, I didn't know the man, so stop treating me like I've committed the crime."

CHAPTER TWO

HANK BARRETT squinted into the bright, September sun. Off in the distance he spotted the familiar black truck driving under the Circle B archway. Brandon. Smiling, he stepped off the back porch to go and greet his eldest grandson. He knew that his fifteen grandkids had better things to do than come visit an old man. But this sure made his day.

Eighty years old on his last birthday, Hank had been blessed with good health. Thankful that he could still climb on a horse, he liked to supervise the ranch work rather than do it these days. And he got to spend time with his three sons, Chance, Cade and Travis. The boys might have been adopted, but he loved them as much as if they were his own blood. No more or less than his own biological daughter, Josie. They all lived close by, and all worked together.

Today with six ranches that formed the Randell Corporation, the operation was far too complicated to work without everyone doing their part. It took all six Randell brothers, along with two cousins, to run things.

Besides family, Hank's main concern these days was to protect the mustangs that roamed the valley here. About a dozen years back he'd made sure the wild ponies would always have a home when he bought up the land to keep it from ever being developed. He wanted the serene Mustang Valley for the wild ponies, his family and the generations to come. Even after he was gone, he trusted his sons to keep that legacy.

God willing, that would be a while longer.

Hank walked toward the dusty truck as Brandon pulled up beside the barn and climbed out. The boy wasn't dressed in his deputy's uniform, but the standard cowboy uniform of boots, jeans and Western shirt.

"Hey, Granddad."

"Hi, Brandon.

A grown man, Brandon didn't hesitate to come up and embrace him in a big hug. Hank liked that.

"What brings you out here, son?"

Brandon knew he hadn't spent much time with Hank lately. He'd been working a lot, trying to make detective. "Does your favorite grandson have to have a reason?"

"Nope. We're just glad you came. Come in and see Ella. I bet she's got something good cooking."

Brandon paused. "Ella's cooking?" It had always been a family joke that their grandmother wasn't good in the kitchen.

Hank grinned. "Yeah. She's been taking a class," he assured him. "And I don't mind sayin' my bride is getting pretty good."

Brandon figured it was more Hank's love for Ella.

He'd finally confessed his feelings about fifteen years ago to his one-time housekeeper. Now, he'd eat anything she put in front of him.

"If you don't mind, could we talk first?" Brandon asked.

Hank gave a nod. "Sure. Why don't I show you the new colt your uncle Chance brought over? We're gonna use him in the big raffle at the rodeo next month."

The Circle B Rodeo had gone on for years, mainly to bring neighbors together to help out with the roundup. The past few years the money from the horse raffle went to the mustang rescue program.

"You're comin' aren't ya?" Hank kept a fast pace as they headed to the barn.

For his age, Hank was in good shape. He stood straight and tall, and his mud-colored Stetson covered a head of thinning white hair. His body was still trim, no extra weight around his waist. His hands might have been a little crippled from arthritis, but it didn't stop him from working.

Brandon smiled. "Isn't it required of all Randells to show up?"

A big grin broke out on Hank's face. "No, just that your dad and uncles are so competitive that they would never miss it." They came to the barn, then Brandon slid open the door and walked inside the cool structure. "And we could always use your help at the roundup. Those greenhorns that pay to come to the guest ranch seem to get themselves lost more often than a stray calf."

Years ago, they had turned the Circle B into a working guest ranch and the roundup was the highlight of the stay.

"So you need backup?"

His grandfather nodded. "Can I include you?"

"I'm starting my new job in a few days, so I'll have to see if I can get the time off."

Hank grinned. "Congratulations. Your dad told me you made detective. We couldn't be prouder of you."

"Thanks."

They walked down the concrete aisle. "I'm not so sure Dad's happy about it," Brandon said. "I think he'd rather I move back home and take over running the ranch."

Hank pulled off his hat and scratched his head. "Well, legally the ranch does belong to you. Nice piece of land, too." He glanced at Brandon. "But I take it your heart's in law enforcement."

Brandon didn't even hesitate. "Yes, it is. It's not that I don't love the ranch, but I'm not into breeding cattle and training horses. Not all day, every day."

They came to the stall in the corner where a nine-month-old chestnut colt was housed. "Hey, fella," Brandon crooned. "How you doing?"

Hank opened the gate and they went inside. His grandfather coaxed the reddish hued animal to his side. "This is Hawk's Flame."

"Oh, man, he's a beaut." Brandon examined the chestnut with the white star on its forehead along with white socks on each leg. "How can Uncle Chance part with this guy?"

"No doubt he's top quality horseflesh. Sired by Flying Hawk. His dam is Crimson Lady."

Brandon should know this, trying to recall the last

time he'd gone to see Uncle Chance and Aunt Joy. That only proved he hadn't been around much. "I guess I've been living in town too long and not paying attention to what's been going on."

"I'm not judging you, Brandon. I think working in law enforcement is commendable, but don't forget your roots, either. Talk with your dad."

"I don't think he wants to hear it right now."

"Maybe if you come up with a plan. Maybe compromise some."

Brandon nodded. That was just it—he didn't have a plan, and now another complication. All he'd been able to think about in the past three days was Nora Donnelly. He'd called the hospital, but she hadn't returned to work.

"I get the feelin' there's something else on your mind," Hank said.

Brandon stroked the horse. "It's a case I've been working on. A woman was attacked in the emergency room parking lot."

"I read about that. How is she doing?"

"She was checked out and released that night." He shook his head. "It's just I have this feeling she knew her attacker."

Hank frowned. "You mean like a husband?"

"No, she's widowed, and she says she hasn't dated anyone since his death, so no boyfriend. That seems strange because she's pretty."

"Pretty, huh?"

Brandon nodded. "Yeah. Even with all the bruises from the attack."

"So she's caught your eye."

Yeah, she'd caught his eye all right. He released a long sigh. "My life just keeps getting more and more complicated."

Hank grinned. "A pretty woman is always a complication, but the right one is so worth all the trouble."

Four days had passed since the attack and Nora wasn't sure what to do. There hadn't been any more threats. No one was hanging around her apartment. No mysterious phone calls. Was the man still watching the hospital? Was he waiting for her to return to work? Had this been Jimmy's sick way of letting her know he'd found her?

Nora walked into her bathroom and examined the fading bruises on her face, only a faint discoloration shading her jawline. A long time ago she'd learned to apply makeup like an expert, hiding her shame and humiliation. She closed her eyes and began to tremble as she recalled that night. The pain had been nothing compared to the fear that her ex-husband might have found her.

Although Jimmy couldn't get his hands on her right now, he had people who would do it for money. She glanced around her furnished apartment. Should she take Zach and leave San Angelo? Their emergency suitcases were packed and in the car. Money and Zach's medication were close by. Although it would be hard to change her location and identity, she was prepared to run again. Anything to stay out of Jimmy's reach. To keep her son safe.

Although she and Zach never talked about their past

life in San Diego, it didn't mean he didn't remember those awful years. She also knew their freedom could be snatched away at any time.

No, she couldn't let Jimmy find them. No matter what she had to do, leave the state, color her hair, anything. He would never take Zach away from her. Nor would she go back to that life. She'd already broken the law to protect her son, and she'd do it again. That's why she'd taken more than money from Jimmy's wall safe. Just some added insurance to keep her and Zach out of harm's way.

The doorbell rang and Nora jumped. She thought about not answering it, but went to look though the peephole and saw Deputy Randell standing on the other side.

Taking a relaxing breath, she opened the door to Brandon Randell. He was dressed in a white shirt, dark trousers and a black cowboy hat. His gun was strapped around his waist and he wore a badge on his breast pocket. He could pass for an old time sheriff. "Hello, Deputy Randell."

"Mrs. Donnelly," he said with a nod.

"I thought we'd finished with the questioning."

"Now that I'm a detective with the department, I've been assigned to your case."

Great. "Has anything new come up?"

"Maybe." He looked past her. "May I come in?"

What could she do, but step aside? After removing his hat, the detective walked in, then stepped into the small kitchen and dropped a folder on the table.

Brandon had rushed over to Nora Donnelly's apartment the second he'd gotten this lead. He was determined to find this guy. He glanced over her face. The makeup hid most of the bruises, but they didn't mar her beauty, either. He motioned for her to sit down. She did and so did he.

"This morning, I went to the hospital and talked with some of the nurses in the E.R.," he began as he opened the file. "It seems that a few days before your attack, you attended a woman who came in with multiple bruises, laceration to her face and a broken arm. All done by the work of her husband."

Nora nodded. "Karen Carlson. She was in bad shape. We had to keep her overnight."

Brandon looked over his notes. "A nurse, Beth Hunt, told me you sat at Karen's bedside because she was so afraid her husband, a Pete Carlson, would come to get her."

Her blue eyes lit up. "Have you found him?"

His heart tripped and he had to glance away to concentrate. "Not yet. But you convinced Mrs. Carlson to go into a shelter."

Nora blinked. "You think it was her husband who attacked me?"

"He could have." Brandon pulled a picture out of the folder. "Does this man look familiar?"

Nora studied the mug shot. "He's burly, but I can't say for sure." She handed it back. "Are you going to arrest him?"

"First, we have to find him. But, yes, he has a long rap sheet. He likes to drink and fight, not caring if it's a man or a woman."

"But he'll be arrested?" she asked again.

He nodded. "For his attack on his wife. I need to talk to Mrs. Carlson, first. Would you be willing to go with me?"

"Isn't that your job, Detective?"

"Under the circumstances, I think she'll be more willing to give me information with you there. Twice before she's dropped the charges against the man."

It hadn't taken much to see that Nora Donnelly was uncomfortable. She didn't trust easily. Was it just him, or all men? Had a man hurt her before? Her husband?

"I don't know how I can help."

"All I want is for you to talk with Karen."

Those large eyes locked with his momentarily. Damn, it was hard not to react to her.

She glanced at the wall clock. "Okay, I'll go, but I'll need to be back before three-thirty. My son will need his medication."

"Is he sick?"

"He's diabetic."

Brandon wasn't sure how to respond to that. That had to be rough for the kid, and the mother. He stood. "Then we'll make sure we're back in time. Even if I have to use lights and siren." He smiled, but she didn't.

Nora stood and went to get a sweater and her purse, then returned to the entry. He reached for the doorknob as she did and their hands touched. She jerked back.

"Whoa, Nora," he said softly. "I'm not going to hurt you. And I'm not going to let your attacker hurt you, either."

Her gaze met his, but she quickly glanced away, murmuring, "Don't make promises you can't keep."

Nora looked out the window of the patrol car. Brandon Randell had kept a conversation going during the twenty-minute drive. She didn't want any small talk, or more questions she couldn't answer. Her life could depend on not letting anyone find out her secrets.

Then Brandon turned off the highway onto a tree-lined road. About a quarter mile up they came to a wrought-iron gate. He stopped, rolled down the window and punched in a code on the keypad, then the gate swung open. He continued along the circular driveway toward a sprawling two-story brick and cedar building with black shutters on the rows of double-hung windows.

"It's beautiful," she breathed. "This doesn't look anything like a shelter!"

Brandon smiled. "It was planned that way." He released his seat belt and climbed out.

Brandon Randell strolled around the car, giving her time to pull it together. The closeness in the car had made her very aware of this man; it was difficult not to be distracted by this good-looking cowboy type.

Nora chided herself for even giving the man a second thought. She opened her door and got out, allowing the cool breeze to brush against her heated face.

A huge fountain adorned with cherub angels caught her attention. The refreshing sound of rushing water had her walking toward the grassy knoll with an array of colorful flowers and shrubs. She looked down to see the plaque that read Abby's Garden. Special thanks to Abigail Randell for her work and dedication to Hidden Haven House."

She felt Brandon's presence behind her. "Is she a relative?"

He nodded. "My mother. She helped design and build this place. It took her nearly twenty years to get it completed."

The night of the attack, Nora had heard the nurses talking about the affluent ranching family that gave back to the community. The topic quickly turned to the handsome Randell men.

Nora stole a glance at Brandon. She couldn't deny that he was good-looking, but she sure wasn't going to do anything about it, either. She had no desire to get involved with a man again, ever.

Together they started up the walkway to the door where Brandon pressed the button on an intercom. After identifying himself into the speaker, he opened the door.

Inside, the walls of the entry area were painted a sea-foam-green, the marble floors were spotless and fresh flowers were arranged on the pedestal table in the center. They crossed the room to a large desk where an attractive, middle-aged woman smiled as she pulled off her glasses.

"Well, hello, Brandon," she greeted and looked at his uniform. "I guess I should call you Detective Randell now."

"Just call me when you bake those delicious oatmeal cookies of yours, Bess."

"You come out and see us more often and I'll see what I can do."

Brandon nodded. "Bess this is Nora Donnelly. She's a nurse at West Hills."

The two women exchanged greetings.

"Is it possible for us to see Karen Carlson?" he asked.

Bess nodded. "She's in the rec hall, but I'll have someone bring her to the garden room so you'll have some privacy."

"Thanks." Brandon placed his hand under Nora's elbow and directed her down the hall. Instead of intimidating her, this man's touch stirred other feelings. Feelings she didn't want to think about right now. If ever. When they came to a door, he opened it and moved aside for her to enter first.

The room was surprisingly large and beautiful. Light blue walls, antique white furniture and plush mushroom-colored carpeting. A floral sofa rested against one wall, on the opposite was a desk in front of a row of French doors. She walked across the room for a better view of a lattice-covered patio with large plants and flowers. Beyond, was a vast green lawn.

"It's breathtaking," she breathed against the glass pane.

There was a knock on the door and Brandon opened it to find Karen Carlson standing on the other side. The woman looked like a frightened deer. Her clothes hung on her thin body, with her bandaged arm in a sling. Her dark blond hair was pulled back in a ponytail. She was only thirty-five, but looked years older.

"I was told to come here," she said nervously.

"Hello, Mrs. Carlson. I'm Detective Brandon Randell with the sheriff's department." He stepped aside. "Do you remember Nurse Donnelly?"

"Hi, Karen." Nora smiled and went to her. "I'm glad you're doing so well."

"Nora." Karen came into the room and gave a hesitant smile. "You came to see me?"

"That and to talk with you," Brandon said as he directed the women to the sofa and they sat down. He swiveled a chair around and took his seat.

Brandon exchanged a glance with Nora. "We were wondering if you've had any contact with your husband."

Karen looked panicked and shook her head vigorously. "Oh, no. He's not supposed to know I'm here. That's the rule. This place has to stay a secret." Her eyes grew large. "They said if I contacted Pete I'd have to take my children and leave. I have nowhere else to go. And I can't go back to him."

Nora wrapped her arms around the woman and held her close. "It's okay, Karen."

"Please, don't let him find me," she cried.

Brandon knelt down in front of Karen. "Pete isn't going to find you," he promised. "You're safe. Your kids are safe." He glanced at Nora. "I just need to find Pete. We thought you might know where to look for him, some places he might go."

Karen sniffed as she pulled back and Brandon handed her a folded white handkerchief from his back pocket.

She wiped her eyes. "When Pete drinks, he goes to a place called The Dark Room."

"The strip club on the west side, off the county road?"

She nodded. "We didn't live too far away. Just down the road at the Wagon Wheel Mobile Home Park."

Brandon took out his notepad. He couldn't look at her as he recalled the shambles of the small trailer. He had no doubt Carlson had taken out more of his anger on the place. "We've checked out your home. There's no sign of your husband. Does he have any other family around?"

"His brother lives in Dallas." Karen gave him the name and address. "They don't get along. He has a friend, Max. He lives at the trailer park also." Karen's gaze met Brandon's. "The sheriff already asked me these questions."

"Nora was attacked outside the hospital a few nights ago."

Karen gasped, and glanced over at Nora's face, her eyes widened as she spotted the faint bruises. "Who would do that to you?"

"We wondered if it could possibly be Pete," Brandon said. "Maybe he knew she helped you when they brought you to the hospital."

A tear rolled down Karen's cheek. "This is my fault." Her chin trembled. "If I'd just stayed…"

"No!" Nora interrupted her. "You can't go back to a man who beat you. He could have killed you, Karen."

"If I hadn't made him so angry."

Brandon touched her hand and felt her tense. He cursed to himself, but checked his own anger at the jerk who did this to her.

"You're not to blame for this, Karen. There's never

a reason for a man to strike a woman. Ever," he stressed. "So from this minute on you think about yourself and your kids. Haven House will help you start that new life—without a man like Pete. But first you have to believe in yourself."

She blinked at her tears and gave him a nod. "Okay."

He smiled. "Good. Now, we're going to find Pete, but you have to press charges this time." He stood, took out his wallet and pulled out two business cards. "Here's a lawyer who's a friend of mind, Brad Ashton. He does pro bono work for the center. He can help you. And here's my card. If you need anything call me."

Karen took the cards. "Thank you." She stood. "If I remember anywhere else Pete could be, I'll let you know." Nora hugged her and they watched as Karen walked out.

The room grew silent as Brandon sat on the edge of the desk. So many emotions surfaced as memories of his own childhood flashed in his head. The years of fear, the fights and his mother's muffled cries in the night. He'd been too young and couldn't do a damn thing about it.

"Brandon?"

He jerked out of his reverie. "What?"

"Do you really think Pete was my attacker?"

"He seems to be the best lead we have. The most logical explanation." His gaze met hers and his breath caught. "Unless you have another idea who it could have been?"

She glanced away. "No, I don't."

He'd bet his new promotion that she was keeping something from him. He checked his watch. "We should head back."

Nora was more than ready to leave. She nodded and started across the room just as the door swung open and a mature woman walked in. Beautiful couldn't describe her. Her auburn colored hair was styled in a blunt cut just below her ears. Her fair skin was as flawless as her trim figure.

Her rich green eyes softened as she looked at Brandon. "Well, I heard rumors that you were here."

"More likely Bess tracked you down." He embraced her and kissed the woman's cheek. "Hello, Mom."

"So you do remember who I am." She stepped back from their embrace, then looked in Nora's direction. "Hello, I'm Abby Randell."

"Sorry, Mom. This is Nora Donnelly. She's helping me with a case I'm working on."

Nora put on a smile. "Nice to meet you, Mrs. Randell."

The older woman took her hand. "Please, call me Abby."

"And I'm Nora."

"Oh, what a lovely old-fashioned name." She looked thoughtful. "I don't know any Donnellys. Are you new in the area?"

She nodded. "A few months."

"Nora is a nurse at West Hills," Brandon answered.

Abby Randell glanced between the two of them and smiled. "You probably don't know many people around here."

"I know a lot of people at the hospital."

"Maybe you and your husband would like to come out to the ranch?"

Brandon sent her a stern look. "Mother."

"I'm a widow. It's just me and my son, Zach."

"I'm sorry. That has to be difficult, especially for your son. How old is he?"

"Zach is seven."

Abby smiled. "I have an idea. It's tradition that the family has a barbecue on Sundays while the weather is warm. There are dozens of cousins, and kids whose parents work on the ranch. This weekend we're hosting it at our place." She gave her son a pointed look. "Actually, it's Brandon's ranch."

"It belongs to the family," he corrected.

Abby smiled. "I bet Zach would love to spend a day on a working ranch."

Nora was caught, knowing her son would love to have some kids to play with. "I'm sure he would."

"Then that settles it. Brandon will bring you out this coming Sunday." Abby Randell then turned and walked out before Nora could change her mind.

Brandon sank onto the edge of the desk. "Welcome to the world of the Randells."

CHAPTER THREE

"FOLLOW through, Zach."

With a nod, the seven-year-old threw the baseball and Brandon managed to field the errant toss. "That's pretty good," he told the boy, and was rewarded with a shy smile.

Brandon knew he should be at the office, following up leads on Carlson's family. Yet, thirty minutes ago when he brought Nora back to her apartment, he hadn't wanted to leave. Not after he saw young Zach Donnelly in the yard, tossing a baseball up in the air trying to catch it. The kid looked lost.

"A little practice and you'll get better in no time."

"I don't have anyone to play with," Zach said, giving his mother a look. "Except Mom."

Nora straightened at her spot on the step. "Hey, I didn't think I was so bad."

"I know." The boy looked embarrassed as he murmured, "But you're a girl."

Brandon had noticed that. A pretty one, too. He bit back a smile. "What about at school?"

The boy glanced away. "I'm new and the kids around here don't want me to play with them."

Brandon felt a tightness in his chest. Zach was small for his age, and on the thin side. Worse, he was the new kid in town.

"Sometimes it just takes a little time to get to know everyone." Brandon tossed the ball back, and the boy managed to get the new oversize glove under it. "Good job."

Zach's smile quickly faded. "Nobody picks me because all the other kids are better than me."

Brandon doubted that, but the new kid often got picked on. He glanced to Nora, watching the interaction closely. "Maybe I could help you."

The boy perked up. "Really?"

Nora had to end this. She stood and walked toward her son. "Zach, we should probably go inside. You have homework."

"Aw, Mom."

She remained persistent. "You also need to get something to eat."

The boy started to argue, but Brandon stepped in. "Zach, it's best to mind your mother. She only wants you to be healthy and strong. We can do this another day."

"Okay," Zach answered, but didn't leave. "When? When are you coming back?"

Wait. Wasn't she the parent here? "Zach, Detective Randell is busy with work. You can't expect him just to drop everything." She made eye contact with Brandon, daring him to challenge her. "Now, you go inside."

Her son finally nodded, then glanced at Brandon. "Thanks for playing catch with me."

"You're welcome," Brandon said and the boy took off up the steps.

Nora was trying hard to hold her temper. She didn't like how Brandon Randell had worked his way into her private life. She had to put a stop to it. Now.

She faced him. Well, darn if he wasn't giving her one of those cocky, how-can-you-resist-me grins. It wasn't going to work on her.

"Look, Detective—"

"It's Brandon, Nora," he interrupted her. "I think we can move on to first names, don't you?"

No! She wanted to scream. "That's the problem, Det—Brandon. I don't think it's a good idea since we have no reason to even see each other again."

He frowned. "I haven't solved your case."

"You don't need me for that. And I've told you everything I remember of that night."

Brandon took a step closer. He wasn't sure if he wanted to shake some sense into her, or pull her into his arms and keep her safe. He'd never felt this protective about any woman before.

"What if he comes back?" he asked. "What if this guy discovers where you live? I have a patrol car drive by at night, but even with security, he could still get to you."

Brandon suddenly saw a flash of fear in her eyes and regretted his harsh words. They tore at his gut. "I'm only trying to say that it won't hurt if this guy knows of my presence here. Think of Zach."

Her fists clenched. "My son is all I think about. That's why I don't want you to get involved in his life. He's already developed a little hero-worship as it is."

Brandon had never been anyone's hero before. "A boy needs another guy around." No one knew that better than he did. He'd been about Zach's age when his mother divorced her jerk of a first husband. "I only want to be his friend, Nora. Is that so bad?"

"What happens when we move away?"

He studied her. Her statement bothered him more than it should have. "Are you planning on leaving?"

Her gaze darted away. "I'm not sure I want to settle here permanently."

"It's only been a few months. Give Tom Green County a chance. I've lived here all my life, and it's a great place to raise a child. Get to know more people. Accept my mother's invitation and bring Zach out to the ranch on Sunday. He can meet the Randell cousins and go horseback riding."

"I don't think—"

"You live on a ranch?"

They both looked up to see Zach standing at the top of the porch stairs. "Zach, I thought I told you to start your homework," his mother said.

"I need help with my math." He looked at Brandon. "Do you really live on a ranch with horses?"

"I don't live there now, but my family does. You're welcome to come out to visit."

The boy's eyes rounded. "Really?"

Brandon nodded. "Really."

"Mom, can we go, please. Please? I want to go riding."

Nora glared at Brandon as he fought a smile. "Okay, but we'll talk about the riding later. Now, go inside. I'll be up in a minute."

Once Zach went through the door, Nora turned to Brandon. "Thank your mother for the invitation. If you give me the time and directions, we can get there."

Brandon grinned. "There's no need. I'll pick you up about noon on Sunday." Before she could argue, he tipped his hat and walked to the patrol car. For the first time in a long while he was looking forward to a visit to the ranch.

Sunday turned out to be a warm, sunny day. From the minute Brandon picked them up, Zach hadn't stopped talking. He asked question after question from the backseat, and Brandon managed to answer every one of them, not once getting upset with the excited seven-year-old.

Nora spent her time looking out the window at the vast countryside. Coming from Southern California, she wasn't used to all the open space. It was kind of nice not to worry about traffic or neighbors close by.

"Look, Mom," Zach cried. "Horses."

They'd turned off the highway and driven along the white split rail fence where several horses grazed in the pasture.

"Those are some of Hank's mustangs," Brandon pointed out.

"You mean those are wild mustangs?" the boy asked.

"Not so wild since my brother, Jay, worked hard to saddle break them. In a few weeks, Hank's going to have an auction to give them good homes."

They drove under an archway that read The Randell Guest Ranch Est. 1933.

"Wow, this ranch is really old," Zach said.

"It sure is." Brandon nodded, feeling pride in his heritage. "My great-grandfather Moreau owned it originally. There were a lot of good years, but sometimes it's hard to make it with only running cattle. So now it's also a guest ranch."

"So people can come and ride a horse like me?"

Brandon drove over the gravel path past the barn. "Yeah, and they can hike around the nature trails and go bird-watching. Some even like to help round up the cattle."

"Wow!" Her son's eyes widened. "I want to do that, too."

Nora was amazed at how at ease Zach was with Brandon. He'd never had a positive male role model before.

"We have to wait and see," she said as she looked ahead to see several out-buildings come into view, along with a large barn and a fenced corral. All were well kept and painted a glossy white.

Brandon pulled the truck up beside another one with the ranch logo printed on the door panel. He got out, opened the back door and helped Zach down from the raised vehicle. Before Nora found her way out the passenger side, Brandon hurried around the truck and helped her.

"Thank you," Nora said, feeling a shock from his

closeness. It had been a long time since she felt a man's tender touch. Yet in the past week Brandon Randell's hands had become very familiar. Their eyes locked and she instantly felt more heat.

"At your service, ma'am," he said hoarsely.

Brandon looked down at Nora. Darn if she didn't look good dressed in her trim jeans and tailored blue blouse.

Normally Brandon didn't have much trouble with women, and being a Randell hadn't hurt, either. That same name had also caused problems. His one serious relationship had been because of who he was. Diana wanted nothing more than to marry one of the heirs to the Randell ranching dynasty. Then she'd walked away when he'd chosen a career in law enforcement. He hadn't felt much liking dating since the breakup.

But Nora Donnelly made him want to change that. "I'm glad you came today."

She glanced away. "Zach needs this."

"What about you, Nora? What do you need?"

She seemed surprised at the question. "To keep my son safe and well."

"And I want to keep you safe, too, Nora."

"Once you find Pete Carlson, I will be. And you won't have to come around any longer."

Before he could respond, Brandon heard his name called. He turned as his parents walked toward them.

"You made it." His mother hugged him, then took Nora's hand. "Nora, I'm happy you could come."

"Thank you for inviting us, Mrs. Randell."

"You're welcome, and remember it's Abby." She

glanced at her husband. "Nora, this is my husband, Cade. Cade, Nora Donnelly."

The two shook hands as Abby glanced down at Nora's son. "And you must be Zach. I'm Abby, Brandon's mother, and this is Cade, his dad. Welcome to the Randell Guest Ranch."

The boy nodded. "Thank you for inviting me. I've never been to a real ranch before."

"Well, then, I'm doubly glad you came today. Why don't I take you to meet some of the other kids." Abby looked at Nora. "There are plenty of older kids to watch out for the younger ones. For now they're in the meeting hall, playing video games. A little later some will probably go riding."

"Oh, boy!" Zach cheered.

Brandon felt Nora tense, but his attention turned to Hank as he also joined the group.

"Granddad," Brandon called.

They hugged, then Hank turned to Nora and smiled. "Well, who's this pretty gal?"

After the introductions, Hank took hold of Nora's hand. "I'm sorry to hear about your accident. How are you doing?"

She blushed. "I'm much better, thank you."

Hank nodded, then lowered his gaze to the boy. "I hear your name is Zach, and you want to ride a horse today."

The seven-year-old nodded.

"Well, you've come to the right place." His granddad looked toward the corral. "There's got to be a pony around here. Let's see, I think Pepper would be the best fit for you." He turned back to Zach. "Now, we need to find you a hat. A cowboy's gotta keep the sun out of his eyes to do his job." He pushed his own hat back off his forehead as he eyed the boy's tennis shoes. "And a pair of boots. We wouldn't want your feet slipping through the stirrups, now would we?"

Zach shook his head again. "I don't have a cowboy hat or boots."

"Not to worry. We have plenty of hats and boots… something's bound to fit you." He leaned down toward the boy. "Now, here's the hard part. We need to get permission from your mother. In my experience, sweetness always works on women. So turn it on, son." He nudged Zach toward his mother.

"Oh, Mom, please, can I go riding? They have a horse for me and everything."

Brandon had to hide his smile. The dark-eyed boy knew how to work it.

Nora sent a worried look at Hank. "You say it's a pony?"

Hank nodded. "Yes, ma'am. Pepper is the gentlest animal on the ranch. The guest kids ride him all the time."

"Okay," she finally said and Zach jumped up and down with excitement.

"We'll stay in the corral," Hank promised. "You're welcome to join us."

"I think I will." Nora started off along with Abby, but Brandon stayed back with his dad.

"Nice-looking woman," Cade said. "Is she what's been keeping you so busy?"

Brandon didn't want to hash it through today. "No, but her case has."

Cade released a long breath. "I understand you're busy, son, but it's time we get together with Jay and Kristin. Make some decisions about the future. How about when your sister comes home from school for the roundup?"

He looked at his dad. Cade Randell had always been bigger than life. All the Randell brothers had been.

Brandon was only seven years old when Cade had returned to San Angelo and learned he had a son. Since that day, Brandon had tried hard to always make his dad proud, but lately it seemed he had fallen short of the mark.

"Since I just started my new job, I'll have to see."

His dad nodded. "Now more than ever we need to settle this legal matter. It's the only fair thing for everyone."

Brandon wanted things to go on as they always had. "Why? Jay is running the place just fine."

Cade's back straightened. "Right now, he's running your place."

He raised his hand to stop any more of his father's protest. "All right. Can we deal with this later? I want to enjoy today."

Cade's expression softened. "I guess you'd rather hang out with a certain blue-eyed brunette than your old man."

Brandon found himself smiling, too. "Yeah, I would."

"Then you best get over there, before Jay starts sweet talking her."

Brandon frowned. "That's never going to happen."

Cade Randell laughed as they walked toward the corral.

* * *

"Look, Mom. I'm riding a horse."

"I see, Zach," Nora called from atop the corral fence. She'd been watching her son since he walked out of the barn in his borrowed boots and straw cowboy hat. She hadn't seen him this happy in a long time.

He sat in the saddle on Pepper. A good-size black and white spotted pony. There were two older Randell kids walking alongside of him, encouraging him. Some younger kids were seated on the corral railing, all cheering Zach on. It was Brandon who led the horse around at first, then handed the reins over to him. Nora held her breath as her son rode the animal around the arena by himself.

Whistles and cheers broke out as he climbed off the pony. Kids ran up to give him high-fives. She blinked back the tears, suddenly realizing how much Zach had missed out on. What kind of life had she made for her son?

She thought back to a few months ago and her life with Jimmy. Although they'd been divorced for nearly two years, he'd never let her go. Along with his threats and abuse, he'd used their son as a bartering tool to keep her imprisoned in the large San Diego home.

It had worked, too. The one good thing had been he didn't have time for Zach. But then things turned volatile toward her son, and she knew she had to do something. So when the opportunity arose, she planned their escape.

There was a commotion at the barn entrance, and Nora watched as Brandon rode into the arena on a beautiful, glistening, black horse. The large animal danced around excitedly as its rider worked to get control. Her gaze was glued to the man who rode confidently and soon had the powerful animal cantering around the corral.

Suddenly a younger version of Brandon climbed up to the top railing and sat down next to her. "Hi, I'm Jay, the show-off's brother. Not only am I better looking and smarter, I can ride a whole bunch better, too." He flashed her a grin that showed off dimples.

"And you have dimples, too," Nora said.

Jay's face reddened as he groaned. "What's with women and dimples?"

"Because they're cute."

Nora turned her head as a teenage girl popped up and swung her jean-clad leg over the railing.

"Hi, I'm Ellie," she said and took a seat, too. "Brandon and Jay's cousin. I'm Chance and Joy's daughter. Chance is one of the original Randell brothers, along with Cade and Travis." The pretty blonde smiled. "I can name all the other uncles and aunts, and the cousins, too, but then I'd have to explain all the sordid family details. And that would take forever. Did you know our grandfather was a cattle rustler?"

Nora was shocked. "Hank?"

The girl shook her head. "No, Jack Randell. Hank took Uncle Chance, Cade and Travis in when Jack went to prison." She wrinkled her nose. "But they've all made up now since Jack came back and needed a bone marrow transplant."

Nora didn't know what to say.

"Hey, short stuff," a familiar voice called. "You writing a book?"

They watched as Brandon rode up on the stallion. Seated in front of him was her grinning son.

"Hi, Mom."

She took a breath. "Hi." She looked at Brandon.

He gave her a reassuring smile. "I've ridden all my life." He held her gaze. "And I won't let anything happen to him."

For the first time in a long time, she found herself trusting a man. "I know."

He winked at her. "Zach, how about a ride around the corral?"

Her son held onto his hat as he glanced up at Brandon. "Can we go fast?"

Brandon gave a mischievous grin. "Maybe."

Before Nora could voice her protest, he made a clicking sound, tugged on the reins and turned the horse. They started around the large pen, soon picking up speed, and then suddenly the horse took off in a gallop. Just as suddenly the horse skidded to a stop in the center of the arena, began backing up and then started turning in a perfect circle. He stopped again and turned in the other direction. When the routine ended everyone cheered and the two rode over to her.

"That was fun, Mom."

"Not so much for me," she murmured, trying to slow her heart rate as she offered her son a smile.

Jay jumped down from the railing and helped Zach off the horse. "You still have the knack, Brand."

Brandon patted the horse's neck. "Shadow is still the best." He looked at Nora as the horse shifted sideways. "It's your turn now."

She shook her head. "No, I'll pass."

"Come on, Mom, it's fun," her son coaxed. "Brandon won't let you fall."

Before she could make a decision, Brandon brought the horse closer. He leaned forward, wrapped his arm around her waist and lifted her off the railing as if she weighed nothing.

"Brandon," she gasped and grabbed him around the neck holding on tightly.

"Don't worry, I got you," he whispered against her ear. "You're okay. Now, swing your leg over the horse."

She managed to do just that and ended up on his lap.

"As much as I like you where you are, darlin'," he said through a tight grin. "I think it will be easier to ride if you sat in the saddle alone." As easily as if it were planned, he lifted her slightly, and slid onto the horse's rump. His arms came around hers, he grabbed the reins and walked the horse to the center of the corral.

"Please, don't go too fast," she said as her hands gripped the saddle horn.

"Our first time we'll take it slow and easy," he breathed against her hair.

Nora was so aware of this man's strength, his heat, it threw her off balance. It wasn't in a fearful way, but definitely an all male way. That truly scared her. "Are you making fun of me?" she asked.

"Never." His voice was husky. "Trust me, Nora. I won't let anything hurt you."

"You can't make that promise."

"How about if I promise to do everything in my power to keep you safe?"

She tried to sit straight so she wouldn't make contact with his chest, but it was impossible. She finally gave up and leaned back against him, enjoying the gentle sway of the horse.

Brandon had trouble not reacting to Nora. The smell of her hair. The feel of her trim body tucked against him. How was a man to keep a clear head? Impossible.

It had been that way from the first time he'd met her. It wasn't wise, either, at least not with her assault case still open. Her attacker was still out there.

What he needed was a clear head, and she clouded his judgment with just a look. Her eyes mesmerized him, her full, pouty mouth made him ache for a taste and her body haunted his dreams. Yeah, he wanted her. Problem was, she didn't want any part of him.

"I take it you've never ridden before."

"Not much of a chance in the city."

"I could teach you and Zach to ride. There's a real pretty spot not far from here, Mustang Valley. There are a lot of mustangs out there."

"That's not a good idea. Zach is diabetic…I have to watch him closely."

Brandon had no idea how hard it would be to deal with a sick child. "I could help you. I know you're a nurse, but I'm trained in first aid."

He felt her hesitation. "Look, Brandon. This was nice of you to invite us out here today, but I'm not looking for a relationship. And it wouldn't be fair to you to lead you on."

She wasn't even giving them a chance. "Why don't you let me worry about me? Besides, I just want to spend time with you and Zach."

"All my time goes on my job at the hospital and the rest is for my son."

"You're here with me now," he told her and glanced over toward the group of kids around her son. He smiled. "Zach looks pretty happy. What would make you happy, Nora?"

When she glanced up at him, he could see the sadness in her eyes. "I don't need anything."

Brandon stopped Shadow at the far end of the corral, away from prying eyes. "Surely you want something, Nora. Maybe I can help."

Those blue eyes filled and she turned away. "No one can help."

His fingers touched her chin, gently turning her face toward him again. "Let me try, Nora. Everyone needs something…somebody." Unable to resist, he leaned forward and brushed his mouth against hers. It was a gentle kiss, but caused her to gasp. Brandon pulled back and saw her surprised look.

"You feel it, too, don't you, Nora?" he said. "There's something happening between us."

CHAPTER FOUR

BEFORE Nora could give her answer, Brandon heard someone calling to them and glanced toward the group along the railing. His brother was waving at him as he held a limp Zach.

"Zach!" Nora cried.

"Hold on," Brandon kicked the horse's sides and they raced across the arena. He slid off the animal to the ground, then helped Nora down.

She ran to her son. "Zach?"

"I'm o...okay, Mom." His words were slurred.

Nora glanced at Brandon. "I need my bag. It's in the backseat of your truck."

Brandon wasn't leaving her. "Jay, go get it. We'll meet you at the house."

As his brother took off along with some of the kids, Brandon scooped Zach up in his arms. "Hey, Zach. How about we go inside where it's cooler?"

"I don't want to go home," the boy insisted weakly.

Brandon kept a fast gait toward the house. "How about we just think about making you feel better, partner."

They met Jay at the porch and held open the door. Brandon carried Zach into the kitchen. His mother sat at the table along with some of his aunts. She stood. "What happened?"

"Zach overdid it a little," he called and continued into the family room. He laid the boy on the cool leather sofa and stood back as Nora went to work.

After opening her oversize bag, she pulled out a meter and quickly tested Zach's blood sugar levels. Then out came the individual packaged tablets. "His blood sugar is low," she explained. "He needs a glucose tab."

Working to slow his pounding pulse, Brandon gave Zach a reassuring wink. He knelt down beside mother and son. "Hey, Zach, it's going to be okay." He brushed the boy's hair back from his forehead.

"I...I lost my hat," Zach said sleepily.

Something tightened in Brandon's chest. He didn't like feeling so helpless. "I bet we can find it."

It took about ten minutes, and Zach began to feel better.

Brandon looked over his shoulder to see his mother standing in the doorway. Holding a glass of orange juice and two bread rolls on a plate, she walked to Brandon and handed it to him.

"Thanks," he said, then looked down at the boy on the sofa. The color returned to his cheeks, and his eyes were brighter. "Are you thirsty or hungry, Zach?"

With a nod, the child sat up, took the glass and drank thirstily. "Thanks," he said as he handed to glass back to him.

"You're welcome, son," Brandon said.

"I'm sorry, I got sick."

It was Abby who spoke. "We're just glad you're okay."

Nora took another meter reading. "It's in the normal rate."

Abby smiled. "Zach, the other kids decided they want to watch a movie before supper. They're saving you a seat in the game room. If your mother will tell me what kind of snacks you'd like, I'll bring them in."

Zach glanced at his mother. "Please, can I go and see the movie?"

Nora frowned. "Zach, maybe we should call it a day."

"But, Mom, I feel okay now. Please."

Teenage Ellie appeared in the room, carrying the missing cowboy hat. "I'll look after him, Mrs. Donnelly. Just tell me what to watch for."

Nora's gaze went to her son. "Okay, but if you start to feel bad, you have to tell me."

"I promise." He sat up slowly and wrapped his arms around her neck. "Thanks, Mom. This is the best day ever." Then he stood and took Ellie's hand. The two walked out together.

"He'll be okay, Nora." Brandon came up behind her, wanting to reassure her. "He's right down the hall and you can check on him anytime."

Suddenly the room emptied out as Nora began to clean up the mess. He could see that her emotions were pretty raw. Since her husband's death, she had to handle her son's illness on her own. He found he wanted to share a little of her burden.

He sat down on the ottoman next to the sofa. "Hey, Nora, Zach's okay now."

She put the test kit into the bag. "I should have been watching him."

"You can't be there every second, Nora. We know the signs to look for now."

She looked at him. "I have to be. I learned a long time ago to only depend on myself."

"You don't have any other family to help you?"

Nora shook her head. "It was just my grandmother, my mother and me growing up. They were both gone by the time I turned fourteen."

That was rough. Brandon reached out and took her hand. "Couldn't you lean on me just a little?"

Her blue eyes widened as she tried weakly to pull her hands away. "I don't lean easily, Brandon. Besides, it wouldn't be fair to you."

"Fair? You think because your son is diabetic that I couldn't handle it? That I wouldn't want to see you again? To get to know you and Zach better?"

"No, it's just that I can't give you what you need. I don't do relationships anymore." She glanced away and he couldn't help but wonder who had caused her to feel this way. Her deceased husband?

"Well, just so you'll know, Nora, Randell men don't give up easily."

Nine o'clock that evening, they were on their way home. Zach had fallen asleep in the backseat of the truck and Nora thought about their near perfect day. She didn't know how to take the Randells. Their generosity, the friendship they'd offered so willing, the honest caring they'd showed to Zach. Her son had been treated no differently than any of the other Randell kids. How could she not want that for him?

Yet she had to resist it—resist the warm, secure feeling of family. Most of all she had to resist Brandon. She touched her lips, remembering the kiss that had thrown her off guard. She also recalled his words. "Randell men don't give up easily."

No matter how much she wanted to spend time with this man, she couldn't. No matter how much she was starting to care for him, she couldn't get Brandon Randell involved in her mess of a life.

"You're awfully quiet," Brandon said from across the dark cab.

"Just relaxing and enjoying the quiet."

"My family can be a bit much." She could hear the smile in his voice. "I think Zach had a good time today."

"The best." She turned toward him, studying his profile. He was a handsome man, but she couldn't get him involved in her mess. "I can't thank you enough for inviting us today, but…"

"Does there always have to be a 'but,' Nora?" He turned down her street. "Can't you just say you enjoyed the day, being together, and maybe even make plans for another time?"

She was afraid to. It wasn't safe for this to go any further. "I can't."

When Brandon pulled up in front of the apartment,

he gave a quick glance over his shoulder at the sleeping Zach. Unfastening his seat belt he moved across the bench seat toward her, and Nora felt the panic.

"Be warned, Nora Donnelly, I'm going to do my best to change your mind," he breathed as he leaned closer.

Nora wasn't afraid of Brandon Randell—not of him hurting her physically, anyway—but her heart was definitely in jeopardy.

Brandon's hand cupped her jaw, and she gasped in anticipation. She couldn't deny she wanted him. Oh, she ached for his tenderness, his touch…his kiss. He didn't disappoint her, either. He captured her mouth and things quickly intensified, igniting heat between them. His tongue touched her lips, parting them and delving inside to taste her. She gripped the front of his shirt, feeling his solid chest under her fingertips, his pounding heart.

With a moan, she moved in closer, pressing her body against his, eager for contact; a connection she hadn't had in so long. God help her, she threw up a prayer, needing guidance. But deep down, she knew she couldn't lose her resolve. Not now. It could mean she'd lose what was most important to her. Her son.

She tore her mouth from his and pushed him away. "Stop!" she gasped. "I can't do this."

His breathing was labored, too. "Okay, it might be too soon."

Nora glanced at the backseat, then at him. The security light shone through the windshield and revealed the intensity and need in his gaze.

She had to turn away. "No, Brandon, it's more than that. We can't start anything."

"We've already started something, Nora. It's been there between us since the beginning."

"Then it's going to stop now." She paused. "I'm sorry. I never meant to lead you on."

He studied her, then finally said, "Who hurt you, Nora? What man made you so untrusting?"

She glanced away, hating the way he'd been able to read her. "It was a long time ago." She shook her head. "And not important anymore."

His finger touched her chin, and turned her back toward him. "It's important to me, Nora, because you're becoming important to me."

Tears filled behind her eyes, but she couldn't let him weaken her decision. She shook her heard. "No, don't say that. You're the detective working on my case. That's all."

A soft sound came from the backseat and Nora felt relieved as her son sat up, rubbing his eyes. "We home?"

"Yes, honey," she told him. "And I better get you to bed. It's getting late."

"Okay, partner," Brandon said. "I guess we have our orders." He gave Nora one last look and climbed out. He opened the back door and unfastened Zach's seat belt, then lifted him into his arms. Nora's heart squeezed, seeing the big man holding her son. Brandon waited for her and together they walked up the steps.

"It was fun today, Brandon," Zach said. "Thanks for taking me to the ranch."

"You're welcome, kid. You'll have to come back for the rodeo."

Nora didn't want Brandon making plans for them.

"Can we, Mom? Can we go to the rodeo?"

Nora unlocked the door, stepped inside and flipped on the light. "We'll have to see, honey."

The boy frowned. "You always say that. It probably means no."

"Zach," she said warningly. "I said we'll see. I only want to make sure you're okay."

Before the boy could argue, Brandon jumped in. "Sounds fair to me," he said. "Now, it's time for bed. Where is your room?"

Nora wanted Brandon to leave, but also didn't want to make a big deal out of it. She pointed down the hall, then went to get her son a pair of pajamas. On her return she heard laughter, and found Brandon had stripped the jeans and shirt off the giggling boy. He took the sleepwear from her and within seconds had Zach dressed for bed.

Just as easily, he hugged the boy, then stood back and let her kiss her son.

"Night, Brandon. Night, Mom," the boy called before rolling to his side.

They called in unison. "Good night, Zach."

Brandon closed the door, but didn't walk away. Instead he reached out and drew Nora into his arms. And God help her, she went willingly. There wasn't any hesitation as he leaned down and captured her mouth. A heated kiss that had her breathing heavily, and set her heart racing. Finally he broke it off.

His eyes were dark and brooding. "Make sure you lock up. Goodbye, Nora." He turned and walked through the door. It took every bit of strength she had not to call him back. She told herself it was for the best.

The following week, Brandon got up from his desk at the sheriff's station and walked around. He was restless. He told himself it was because he wasn't used to being cooped up inside. For the past four years, he'd been out cruising in a patrol car. Now as a detective he didn't have that luxury. Seemed a lot of their work was done on the computer, or by phone.

He glanced out the window. He also had too much time to think. And lately there had been far too many distractions. In another week he had the big powwow with the family to come up with a solution for the ranch situation.

To be honest, it had been Nora Donnelly who had kept him awake. He missed her. More than even he wanted to admit. The day at the barbecue had been the best for him. He thought she'd felt the same, but he'd been wrong. And he couldn't do a thing to change her mind.

His phone rang and he went to his desk and picked up the receiver. "Randell."

"Brandon?"

He smiled, hearing his mother's voice. "Hi, Mom? How are you?"

"I'm fine, but your father had an accident."

His throat grew dry as his heart rate picked up. "What is it?"

"He got tangled in some barbed wire."

"How bad?"

She sighed. "Well, he didn't argue when we brought him to the hospital. We're at West Hills."

"I'll be there in ten minutes."

Brandon grabbed his hat, and rushed out, stopping at the dispatcher's desk to tell him of situation. When he got into the car he found his hands shaking. He drew a calming breath, telling himself that his dad would be okay. He was strong and healthy. He started the car, feeling the emotions well up. He hadn't felt that way since he'd been seven years old, and Cade Randell had called him son for the first time.

Nora looked at the name Randell on the chart. Her heart raced, thinking about Brandon. It didn't slow seeing the first name, Cade.

She walked into the cubicle to find Cade Randell seated on the bed, holding onto his arm wrapped in the bloody towel. Abby was close at his side. There were also two other men in the tight space: Cade's brothers, Chance and Travis.

Abby glanced in her direction. "Oh, Nora. Good. We're so glad you're here." She smiled and crossed the room.

"Hello, Abby. Cade." She nodded at the brothers.

"Hi, Nora," the Randell men chorused back.

She went to the bed and unwrapped Cade's injured arm to see several lacerations, tearing deep into the skin. "How did this happen?"

"My brother tangled with some barbed wire," Chance

said, tossing her that infectious Randell grin. "You'd think after all these years he'd know how to string wire."

Cade frowned. "You can leave anytime, bro," he told him. "In fact, you both can go…I'm in the capable hands of these women."

That got rude comments from the brothers as Nora continued to examine more wounds on Cade's arm and back. Then she took his vitals.

"Abby, how did you put up with this man all these years?" Travis said.

Brandon's mother gave her husband a secret smile. "It's been a cross to bear, but I've managed."

Nora could see the couple managed very well. It was obvious in their eyes how much these two loved each other. She almost felt like she was intruding on their private moment.

Nora heard a commotion, then suddenly the curtain was jerked back and Brandon stood on the other side. His eyes showed concern as he looked at his father. "Dad?"

"Hey, son." Cade grinned. "What are you doing here?"

"Mom called." He never took his gaze off the blood on Cade's arm.

His dad groaned and leaned back against the pillow. "I'm never going to live this down."

Travis grinned. "Probably not, but think about the cool scars you're going to have."

"Out," Abby ordered, motioning toward her brothers-in-law. "We need to give Nora room to work. And you guys are irritating the patient."

Travis started for the exit, but not before he joked,

"Hey, Cade would ride roughshod over us if we'd been lying in the bed."

Brandon's nerves calmed seeing his father wasn't in too bad shape. He walked to the other side of the bed and hugged his mother, giving him the perfect view of Nora at work. She looked professional, with her hair pulled up in a ponytail. How could anyone look sexy in baggy scrubs? Nora did. Then she turned that blue-eyed gaze on him.

"Hi, Brandon."

He worked his throat. "Nora." He quickly turned away. "Do you need anything, Dad?"

Cade groaned. "Yeah, to be twenty years younger and half a step faster, so I could have gotten out of the way."

He couldn't figure out what his dad was doing stringing barbed wire in the first place? Hadn't they hired ranch hands to do that?

Before Brandon could ask, a doctor walked in and asked everyone but Abby to leave. Brandon was almost relieved to step outside and went to the waiting area along with his uncles.

"Hey, don't look so worried," Chance said as he hugged him. "Your dad is made of strong stuff. He'll be just fine, especially with your pretty nurse taking care of him."

"She's not my pretty nurse," Brandon denied.

Travis joined them. "Oh, boy, haven't we all said that before." He wrapped his arm around his nephew's shoulders. "So what's with all those sparks flying around in there?"

Brandon ignored him.

Chance sobered. "Give it some time, son."

"I don't think time is going to change Nora's mind."

"No, but you can," Chance said. "Besides, since when have Randell men ever done anything the easy way?"

CHAPTER FIVE

HOURS later, after his dad had been released from the hospital and was back home, Brandon returned to West Hills. His work shift had ended and he'd been on his way to his condo when he thought about Nora. She'd be leaving work in the dark, alone, and that was all it took for him to head to the hospital.

It had only been a couple of days since she'd gone back to work. He told himself that he wanted to make sure she was being escorted to her car, but he didn't want her to know about the visit. If she caught him, he could tell her that he wanted to check out the parking lot security. Worst case, she wouldn't believe him and have him arrested for stalking her. It was worth the risk, especially since they hadn't found Carlson, yet.

Brandon parked his truck and headed toward the emergency entrance, but stood off to the side. After a while a group of nurses came through the automatic doors. Nora wasn't one of them. Then another group walked out, but she wasn't with them, either.

Brandon finally approached a nurse he recognized from earlier questioning. "Excuse me, Megan isn't it?"

The cute blonde smiled at him. "Well, hello, Detective Randell. What brings you back here?" Her smile dropped. "Did something else happen?"

"No. So far everything is fine. Just checking to make sure you ladies are getting to your cars safely."

"Isn't that nice of you."

"It's my job, ma'am." He glanced around. "I don't see Nora Donnelly. Has she left work yet?"

"I saw her in the nurses' locker room." Megan glanced over her shoulder. "She should be coming out soon."

"Thank you," he said as a security guard walked to the group. "Looks like your escort is here. Have a nice night." He tapped his finger to his hat, then headed toward the doors.

He didn't care anymore that Nora knew he was there. All that mattered was that she got safely to her car.

Nora pulled her sweater and purse out of her locker and closed it. She was exhausted, but it was a nice tired. It felt good to be back at work. The only downside had been seeing Brandon. Since they'd parted company earlier today, she hated that she hadn't been able to put the man out of her head. After one kiss, he was slowly working his way into her head, and her heart.

As hard as she tried she couldn't stop thinking about the way he'd kissed her. How he'd lavished close attention to her mouth, driving her to distraction so she couldn't even think clearly.

No! She had to put Brandon Randell out of her mind. She slammed her locker door and jerked on her sweater. Maybe the best thing for her to do was not to risk fate and just move on. Away from a man she could never let get too close to her. She couldn't entangle Brandon in her mess of a life. If Jimmy found out...

She walked past the rows of lockers, through the door and into the deserted hallway at the back end of the hospital. Suddenly the stairway door opened and out stepped a man dressed in green scrubs. She didn't recognize him since his head was down, but the fact that he wasn't wearing a badge set off her weariness. She picked up her pace, but didn't get far.

She let out a loud gasp for help as he gripped her by the arm and jerked her into the stairwell. She fought him but he was too strong. "Please, let me go," she cried.

"Shut up. I'm not going to hurt you if you behave."

Her rapid heart rate and her intuition told her differently. She glanced around for an escape, praying someone would come into the stairs.

He backed her against the wall. "I just need to talk to you, Nora Donnelly."

Oh, God! He knew her name. "Please, I have to get home."

"And you will as soon as you tell me where Karen is."

She stole a glance at his face. The man in the picture Brandon had showed her. Pete Carlson. "I don't know where she is, Mr. Carlson. You need to check with the hospital."

In a flash, he grabbed her arm again. She gasped.

"You're lyin'." He snarled through his teeth. She smelled alcohol. "You were with her the night she came here."

Nora tried to pull away. "I don't remember," she lied again, praying that someone would come by. Her thoughts turned to Zach. She had to get away.

"Yes, you do," he hissed. "This is all your fault. It was you who told Karen to leave me," he said through clenched teeth.

"Carlson! Take your hands off her!"

Nora jerked her head around to see Brandon in the doorway, his gun pointed at them. Suddenly her legs gave out and she slid to the ground, breaking the man's hold. Her assailant took off down the steps.

Brandon ran up to her. "Nora, are you okay? Did he hurt you?"

"I'm fine. Please, just get him."

"I will," he told her as he helped her to her feet. At the same time the security guard showed up. "Don't leave until I get back."

Brandon called for backup as he hurried through the emergency room and outside. He glanced around and saw a figure running for the back lot. Calling for another security guard, together they ran up the rows of parked cars. He wasn't going to lose this guy. Several yards ahead, he spotted a figure dash between two cars.

In pursuit, he heard the siren and finally the cruiser pulled up in the aisle. Deputy Griggs jumped out and caught up with him.

Brandon wasn't going to stop. This guy wasn't going to get away. He continued to search between each car until he finally lucked out and saw a pair of boots sticking out under a large truck.

He took cover and pulled his gun from its holster. "Okay, Carlson. Let's make this easy."

No answer.

"C'mon, I know you're behind the truck. You have nowhere to go, so don't do anything else foolish. If you have a weapon lay it down and kick it out, then come out with your hands locked behind your head."

He was met with more silence.

Brandon glanced to his right to Griggs. He motioned for the deputy to stay while he circled around to the other side of the vehicle. The overhead lighting was dim, but he could make out a figure crouched behind the truck.

Brandon moved silently as he trained his .45 on him. "Try anything, Carlson, and I guarantee it will only turn out badly."

"Okay! Okay!" The man slowly raised his hands in the air, and Brandon and Griggs moved toward him. They had him against the car, and patted him down for weapons, then Griggs cuffed him.

They walked the suspect back to the patrol car. "I wasn't going to hurt her," Carlson swore. "I wouldn't hurt her. I just wanted to know where Karen is."

Brandon had to work hard to control his anger. "You use your wife as a punching bag, and you want to know where she's gone? How about anywhere away from you?" Brandon placed his hand on top of the man's head and pushed him into the backseat of the patrol car. "Just get out of my face." He slammed the door shut and looked at Jason. "Take him to the station. I'll be by later to help with the report."

The deputy nodded and Brandon marched off. Now that they'd captured the guy, his thoughts turned to Nora. He went inside the emergency room, searching around the waiting area until he found Nora with one of the security guards next to her. She looked lost sitting in the cold plastic chair, a cell phone against her ear. Probably telling Millie she would be late.

By the time he reached her, she'd hung up as he questioned the guard about how the assailant had gotten into the hospital. The guy didn't have any answers.

Nora stood, her eyes wide. "Did you catch him?"

"Yes."

A single tear trickled down her cheek and it was like an arrow to his heart. He hated to see women cry, and also knew what it cost Nora to let him see her weakness.

"Thank, God," she breathed.

Brandon wanted to be relieved, too, but every emotion he had was churning inside him. Nora wasn't just another victim to him. He couldn't continue to make this about the job. And in his head, he couldn't stop thinking about how this could have turned out much differently.

His anger surfaced. "What were you doing by yourself?"

"I needed to talk to my supervisor. I had no idea someone was going to be in the stairwell."

Brandon's fists were clenched. "If I hadn't showed

up…" He turned away. He stopped pacing and returned to her. "Did he hurt you?"

She shook her head and more tears filled her eyes. He cursed again as his hands dropped to her shoulders, then down her arms. She felt too delicate to carry so many burdens. It was over now. "I don't know what I would have done if…"

He drew her against him, and immediately felt her trembling. He brushed a kiss against her hair, and held on; more for himself.

"I was so scared, Brandon." She gulped and made a sobbing sound.

"Shh, it's okay. It's over and you're safe now." He tried not to think about what could have happened if he hadn't showed up tonight. He pulled back and their gazes locked. Even with her haunted look, he read a connection that set off sparks. A surge of heat shot through him.

Nora glanced away. "I hate feeling like this. Not having control."

"It's over." He wanted to be the one she leaned on, the one to protect her.

"Thank you." She sighed. "I'll get Harry to take me to my car."

"No, I'm walking you out. I'm going to make sure you get home."

She didn't argue.

He placed his hand against her back and together they walked out the door. He was glad for the cool air, hoping it would clear his head.

"Do I need to give a statement or something?"

"Yeah, but tomorrow is soon enough." God, he didn't want to let her out of his sight tonight, or tomorrow, or ever.

They arrived at her small sedan. She turned around, her eyes large, questioning.

"Brandon. Why were you at the hospital?"

He held her gaze. "Why do you think, Nora?" He gripped her by the arms, leaned down and kissed her.

His arms wrapped around her as his mouth moved over hers. Slow and deliberate, he wanted to taste her until he got his fill. But that wouldn't happen in this lifetime. He finally broke off the kiss and took a step back.

"Make sure you lock your doors, and wait until I get my truck here to follow you home."

"But the guy's been caught."

"Humor me. You're still shaky. I just want to be sure you get home all right."

She started to open her mouth, then nodded. "Okay."

Nora climbed inside her car and started the engine, then rolled down the window. "It's not that I don't appreciate it, Brandon, but you can't keep coming to my rescue."

Oh, Lord, save him from stubborn women. "Let's hope this is the last time."

The next morning, Nora sat in her kitchen. She felt secure knowing her attacker was caught, and in jail. That she and Zach were truly safe now. It was an even bigger relief that the assailant was Pete Carlson. Sick as it might be, the man wanted revenge because she'd helped his wife. Was there any reason to doubt it?

There was no reason to think Jimmy was after her. Wrong. She didn't doubt for a minute that her ex-husband would try to track her down until the day he died...or she did. That had been Jimmy's promise to her if she ever left him. She'd done so much more than leave him. She stole from him. Not only money and his son, but something even more valuable. It was the only insurance she had to fend off the madman she had once been foolish enough to marry.

One problem solved, but another one had popped up. She glanced down at the letter from the bank. They'd tried calling her yesterday but couldn't reach her. Apparently someone had tried to hack into her account. They'd succeeded in taking a few hundred that she'd kept for bills. Nora kept most of her cash on hand. In case she had to get away, and so there wouldn't be any trail. The same thought nagged at her. It could be Jimmy.

Millie Carter carried her coffee mug to the table and sat down. "Are you sure you don't want me to go along with you to the sheriff's station?"

Nora glanced at her neighbor. "No, I have to stop by the bank and run several errands. Besides, you need time for yourself."

The older woman sipped her coffee. "Yeah, I can't miss those great deals on the Home Shopping Network."

Nora grinned. "You never know when you might need something for a hot date."

The woman made a rude sound. "The only one who has a worse social life than me is you." A twinkle lit up

Millie's kind hazel eyes. "Of course I have faith Detective Randell can turn that around."

Nora sighed and put down her coffee mug. "I don't have time to date, Millie. Besides, my relationship with my husband—"

"Wasn't as perfect as you want everyone to think," Millie finished.

Nora lowered her gaze. Millie had never asked many questions. If inquisitive, she hadn't shown it. Over the past few years, Jimmy made sure her friends had been discouraged to come around. Millie Carter was a rare find. "I can't talk about it."

"You don't need to say a word, Nora. I only want you to know that one man shouldn't keep you away from finding another. There are some good guys out there." She smiled fondly. "And I think Brandon Randell is one of them."

The older woman looked thoughtful. "I knew Brandon's daddy from school. Cade was as wild as they came back then, but every girl wanted his attention, not to mention the other Randell bad boys, Chance and Travis. They all had problems living down their daddy going to prison."

Nora knew all too well about having a past she'd like to forget. She brightened. "I didn't know you knew the Randells."

Millie waved her hand. "I doubt any of them re-member me. They went for pretty girls like you." She took a sip of her coffee. "And your Brandon is defi-nitely smitten."

A shiver went through her. "Stop it. I can't get involved with any man. I need all my focus on Zach."

"There's no reason why you can't do both."

Nora could think of one big one. "I should get to the sheriff's station." She took her mug to the sink, and got her jacket and purse. Together the two women walked out.

"I'll see you after your shift tonight," Millie said as she went to her apartment two doors away.

Nora had started down the steps when she saw Brandon leaning against a patrol car. She immediately felt a rush of excitement. He looked so good in his crisp, white shirt, fitted khaki pants and polished boots. He tipped his hat to her in that polite Texas way.

A smile creased his strong, handsome jaw. Goodness the man was gorgeous. Her gaze collided with his dark eyes, then moved to his mouth. Memories of his kiss filled her head, causing heat to flood to her cheeks, and other places.

"Nora."

"Brandon," she managed as her heart rate did a double-take hearing his deep voice. "What are you doing here?"

"That seems to be your favorite question."

"Are you following me again?"

He pushed away from the car. "I wanted to make sure you're okay and to give you a ride to the station."

"I should drive myself. I need to go to the bank, too."

"We can stop by there first."

He came closer and she could feel his strength, that sense of protection he gave her. But something in his expression bothered her. "Is there something else you need to tell me?"

"There might be a slight problem."

She waited. "What?"

"Carlson swears he wasn't anywhere near the parking lot last week, that he never attacked you."

Nora's heart skipped a beat then started racing. Oh, no. "It's got to be him."

Two hours later, Brandon had finished taking Nora's statement and sent her out for her signature. She hadn't been able to identify Carlson as the man who'd attacked her the previous week. They still had to confirm the suspect's alibi before they could move ahead with anything.

The good thing was that Carlson had already been charged for the assault on his wife, and he couldn't make the bail. So for now, he remained in jail. Brandon hoped Karen Carlson wouldn't back down on her promise to testify against her husband. Too many women never went through with it. Even his own mother had stayed with her jerk of a first husband, Joel Garson. Brandon had been grateful every day since she'd packed them up and left.

His cell rang, and he checked the ID, seeing the ranch's number.

"Hello."

"Brandon," his mother said.

"Hi, Mom. How's Dad?"

"Impossible. Bullheaded. Stubborn."

Brandon smiled. "Giving you a bad time, is he?"

"He won't stay in bed, or take his painkillers. In other words, he's driving me crazy. Do you think you could stop by?"

"And what? Hold a gun on him? I don't think that's going to work, either."

"Well, something better. He's going to pull out his stitches."

Great. "Does he need to go back to the doctor?"

She sighed. "You and what army is going to take him?"

Brandon checked his watch and glanced through the glass partition to see Nora. "Just a minute, Mom." He went to the doorway. "Nora, my dad is having some trouble with his stitches and he won't go to the doctor. Do you think you can take a look at them?"

She glanced at the clock. "I guess I have time."

"Thanks, I owe you," he told her.

She gave him a half smile, lighting up those sapphire-colored eyes. "I believe I owe you a few favors."

He could conjure up a lot of things he'd like to ask her for. But he thought it would be wise to keep his mouth shut, and just enjoy the time he was going to get to spend with her.

Brandon heard his father's loud voice the minute he opened the back door. He wasn't sure they shouldn't turn around and leave.

He turned to Nora. "Come on, but be ready to duck flying objects."

Brandon led the way into the great room to find his shirtless father pacing around. His mother had her arms folded across her chest, glaring at her husband. He was used to his parents' heated arguments, but he also knew of their passion for each other. He wanted the same kind of marriage.

The room grew silent. "Now comes the standoff," Brandon said.

Both his father and mother turned to him. Abby smiled. "Brandon, Nora, good you're here."

Cade glared at his wife. "So you called for reinforcements. That's really underhanded, Abby."

"I don't play fair when it's about your health. You wouldn't go to the doctor, so Brandon brought Nora out here."

Nora didn't hesitate; she simply marched across the room to Cade Randell. She smiled, and Brandon felt jealous it was directed at his father.

"Hello, Cade," she said. "I hear you've had some trouble with your wounds."

Brandon watched in amazement as his father's expression softened. "Nothing to worry about," Cade said. "But I'm wrapped up so tight I can't even move."

Nora raised an eyebrow. "Maybe I can help with that. Would you mind if I had a look?"

Cade shrugged. "Why not? I won't get any peace around here until you do." He walked to the ottoman and sat down.

Nora quickly washed up in the connecting bathroom. On her return, she went to work and began removing the bloodstained bandages around his father's torso and shoulder. His mother came into the room with a large emergency kit. She opened it, but didn't hang around. She walked out. "Come on, Brandon, help me make some lunch."

Brandon had always thought the kitchen was the best part of this big, old house. It had been remodeled about five years ago. Rich cherrywood cabinets lined the walls, with solid granite countertops the color of sand with sparkles of rich brown tones. An oversize farmer's sink sat under the window that overlooked the ranch's center of operations: the barn and corral.

He pulled out a high-back chair and sat at the long table. "Has dad been like this since you brought him home?"

She nodded. "He isn't taking anything for the pain, either. That's okay, but he has to stay still at least for a few days." She opened the refrigerator and pulled out a platter of ham. "He tried to ride out with Jay this morning."

Suddenly his father's laughter rang from the other room and his mother raised an eyebrow. "Should I be jealous of Nora?"

"Right now, I'm jealous of Dad."

His mother came to the table. "You're so much like him. Oh, you might not have Cade's rough edges, but you have the same seriousness, the same loyalty to your beliefs, and the people you love." She touched his jaw. "Have I told you how proud I am of you?"

He nodded. "I've always known that."

His mother sat down next to him. "I like Nora."

"So do I." He sat back with a sigh. "I just wish she liked me a little more."

Abby raised an eyebrow. "She has a lot to deal with. She lost a husband at a young age, and her job is demanding, and her son... Zach's condition has to be a struggle." She faced him. "A lot of men would walk away from that situation."

"Why? Zach's a great kid. He's just having some trouble adjusting to his medication."

Tears filled his mother's eyes.

"What?"

She shook her head. "Oh, Brandon, you're definitely one of the good guys." She leaned over and kissed him.

"Great. I get kisses from my mother."

"Be patient and I'm sure you'll get plenty of kisses from someone else."

"Are you sure about that?"

His mother smiled. "If you don't come on like a gangbuster. Give Nora some space. If she's guarded, she might have good reason to be."

There was more laughter from the other room. "Except maybe around your father, but that means she's starting to trust you, too, because we're your family. Of course, you daddy is a pretty good charmer."

Brandon knew he could rely on Abby Randell's insight. He, too, had picked up his own signs that something in Nora's past had kept her from being too trusting with people.

His mother's green eyes locked with his. "Nora needs to be convinced that you'll stick around when things get rough." She placed her hand on his. "But I think you've already decided that."

"It would be smarter not to be involved, but with Nora Donnelly I can't seem to help myself."

CHAPTER SIX

LATER that night, Nora drove home after her shift ended at the hospital. It was nearly ten o'clock and she was tired. Another long day. Normally tomorrow would be her day off, but the hospital was short-handed, so she'd volunteered to help out. She couldn't afford to turn down the extra money, in case she had to move on quickly.

Thinking of money. She still had to go to the bank in the morning to have her funds released. It was a good thing she'd kept cash on hand. That way she didn't leave anything to trace.

Nora drove down the street and parked in her space. After turning off the engine, she sat for a moment. Was her account getting compromised just a coincidence, or had Jimmy found her? Was he playing with her? She didn't have any proof that he'd found her. Rey Alcazar, aka Jimmy Archer, was in jail awaiting trial and if she were lucky he'd be sent to prison for a long, long time. Until then she had to be vigilant. That meant she couldn't get involved with anyone. No more afternoons spent with Brandon, or having lunch with his family. If Jimmy learned the connection he would hurt them.

Yet, for a few hours today she'd relaxed, even fantasized about how it would feel to be part of a family like the Randells. Where Zach could feel loved and secure.

Her thoughts turned to Brandon. She couldn't let herself think of him as anything other than the detective working on her case. She couldn't even dream about someone like Brandon in her life, or how easily it would be to fall for him. No, she couldn't let this go any further. Now that Pete Carlson had been caught, there wasn't any reason for her to see him again.

She climbed out of her car and walked to her apartment. After unlocking the door, she went in, but stopped short on seeing Brandon in her kitchen. Her son, dressed in his pajamas, was seated across from him eating a bowl of cereal.

Brandon saw her first. With a smile, he stood. "You're home."

"Mom, hi," Zach said as he got up and hurried to her.

For a second it seemed the most natural thing in the world for both of them to greet her. Yeah, if it were a perfect world.

Nora hugged her son. "Hey, what are you still doing up? And where's Millie?"

"She got sick and started throwing up. A lot," Zach told her. "So I called Brandon and he came over."

"Oh, Zach, you should have called me." She looked at Brandon. "I'm sorry he bothered you."

"It's not a bother, Nora. You came out to check on my dad today. Is this any different?"

It was different since she'd just sworn off the good-looking cowboy. "It's still an inconvenience."

"Not for me. We've been having a good time, right, Zach?"

He nodded. "Yeah, Mom. We played Star Wars and watched a video. It was fun."

She smiled, stealing a look at Brandon. "I bet it was."

"It was fun," Brandon confirmed. "I happen to like Star Wars."

She turned back to her son. "How are you feeling?"

"I'm fine. I showed Brandon how to test my blood sugar." The boy shrugged. "He said he wanted to learn."

"So everything is okay?"

The boy nodded. "Yeah, Millie helped me with my shot before she got sick."

"Okay, then, it's time for you to be in bed."

Her son started to argue, but exchanged a glance with Brandon. "Sure, Mom. Can Brandon read me a story?"

She felt a twinge of hurt, then realized how much her son needed male attention. She studied the man dressed in jeans and a dark T-shirt, and her pulse shot off. She wouldn't mind some of his attention herself.

She felt heat rise to her cheeks. "Maybe you should ask Brandon."

"Sure," he said. "But go brush your teeth, then give a shout when you're in bed."

They both watched Zach run off. Brandon turned to Nora. He wasn't sure how she'd take to him being here.

One thing was for sure, she looked tired. With reason, after spending eight hours on her feet. But take his help? He wasn't so sure she would.

"Millie was going to call you, but when I got here, she was pretty weak. I was more concerned about getting her home."

"So when my son called you, you came running."

He smiled and nodded. As far as Brandon could guess Nora Donnelly hadn't gone out of her way to get to know many people. Millie Carter was pretty much it. "There wasn't anyone else listed. He trusted me enough to call."

She sighed. "I just don't want Zach to keep calling you whenever he feels like it. He's taking advantage."

Brandon wished the boy's mother would take advantage of him. "I told you both to call me anytime." He took a step closer. "Don't you understand, Nora? I want to be that guy. I want to spend time with you, and with Zach."

She crossed her arms over her chest. "And I told you it isn't a good idea."

She stared up at him with those rich blue eyes, and he could see that she was denying the truth. He could see that his closeness was affecting her, too.

He wanted to push it further. "Then this probably isn't, either."

As Brandon dipped his head, her rapid breath fanned his cheek and fueled his desire. His hands cupped her face, his thumbs sliding over the smooth, pale skin of her cheeks. Her eyes grew wide, her throat worked to swallow, but she didn't pull away.

"But I can't seem to resist you," he whispered. Then he claimed her mouth with his, lips moving over hers, gently at first. Hearing her soft moan, he gave himself up to the need within and deepened the kiss. He parted her lips, sweeping his tongue into her warmth, exploring her secrets. He felt each and every breath, rushing in and out of her lungs. She clung to him, and gave back everything he asked for. And it wasn't enough. He wanted more.

He needed more.

They were both gasping by the time he finally released her. Still holding her, Brandon rested his chin on top of her head, and fought to steady his own heart rate. When he felt capable of forming words, he finally added. "Woman, you pack a wallop."

She slipped from his embrace. "I didn't mean for that to happen."

He couldn't help but grin. "Darlin' it was bound to happen. You and me, we're explosive together."

Nora didn't deny it, but she didn't have to like it. "I should check on Millie." She began backing up and bumped into the counter, but still couldn't take her eyes off the man who was turning her brain into mush. "Could you watch Zach for just a while longer?"

"As long as you want. I'll be here waiting," he promised.

That was what she was afraid of. "Thanks," she managed before she grabbed her keys and left.

In the cool night, she leaned back against the closed door to catch her breath. What had she done? She touched her mouth. She could still feel and taste Brandon. The sin of it was, she wanted more than anything to go back for more.

She wanted Brandon Randell.

"Why did you kiss my mom?"

Brandon's head shot up from the storybook he'd been reading. The inquisitive seven-year-old was tucked into the twin bed, waiting for an answer.

Brandon usually wasn't at a loss for words. Until now. He'd never dated anyone with a child before. Technically he wasn't dating Nora.

"Well… I like your mom."

"But she's a girl." The boy said it like it was a disease. "You like kissing girls?"

Brandon had to work not to smile. "I didn't at seven, but I do now. If she's the right girl."

The boy's dark eyes turned thoughtful. "And Mom's pretty, too."

"Zach, does it bother you that I like your mom?"

He rubbed his hand under his nose. "Not if you're nice to her. I don't want you to be mean like he was."

That immediately alerted Brandon. "Someone was mean to her?"

The child glanced away and shrugged. "I'm not supposed to talk about it, 'cause he scares me."

Brandon tensed. He couldn't handle men who picked on women and children. "Did he hurt you?"

"No, Mom didn't let him. But he hit her and it made me cry."

Brandon had to work hard to hide his anger. "Who did this, son?"

The boy hesitated, then said, "My dad. But he's not my dad anymore."

Brandon was almost happy the guy was dead. "Look, son, you don't have to worry about me ever hurting your mom. I promise you I would never lay a hand on her or you. I care about you both."

All at once it struck him what he was promising. These two were becoming important to him. He wanted to take care of them. As if Nora would let that happen. "Now, I think it's time you go to sleep."

The boy didn't move. "Do you think seven is too old to hug?"

Brandon gave an exaggerated frown. "You're never too old for hugs." Brandon wrapped his arms around the boy's small frame. His chest tightened and a feeling went through him that he couldn't describe, but it was all good. He also remembered being Zach's age when his dad came into his life. Cade's love gave him a secure feeling like he'd never had before. He wanted Zach to feel the same.

Brandon released Zach, tucked in the blanket and whispered good-night and closed the door. He pulled out his cell phone and punched the number he'd memorized as a child. On the second ring, the familiar deep voice answered.

"Hello, son," Cade Randell answered.

"Hi, Dad," he said, a little hoarseness in his voice.

"Is something wrong?"

No, everything was right. "I just wanted to know how you were doing."

"Much better now since your lady fixed me so I can move around. I like her, Brandon."

"I like her, too."

There was a pause. "So this is serious."

He didn't even have to think about it. "I can't seem to convince her of that, but I'm working on it."

"Your mother didn't exactly make it easy for me, either. It took a lot to win her. We were both pretty stubborn. But I have to say it was definitely worth it."

Brandon leaned against the wall. It felt good to talk with his dad. They used to do it all the time. When had it stopped? "Got any ideas on what I can do?"

"Yeah. Since I won't be able to team up with Travis in the calf roping event at the rodeo, I told him you'd go in my place."

Brandon groaned. "Dad, I haven't done any roping in years. I'll make a fool of myself."

"Come on, son. You're a Randell—it comes natural to you."

Nora walked in just as Brandon closed his phone. She wasn't sure what to say.

Brandon finally spoke. "How's Millie?"

"Terrible, but she's finally keeping some tea and toast down. She's feeling too bad to watch Zach tomorrow. I need to call work." She went to the phone, but his words stopped her.

"Hey, I'm off tomorrow. I can watch Zach."

She shook her head. "No, I can't ask you to do that."

He crossed the kitchen. "You didn't ask, Nora, I offered. If you're worried about my experience, I was eight years old when Jay was born, then only a little older when my sister, Kristin, came along. I watched them both."

Nora knew it wasn't the same thing. "But Zach has to be monitored."

"I know. He needs insulin to help regulate his blood sugar. I took EMT training, I can administer a shot."

Brandon Randell was definitely working his way into her life. Problem was, she was letting him.

"Nora, have I given you any reason not to trust me?"

Trust had never come easy for her. "Of course not. It's just you're spending far too much time with us…and I can't let that happen."

"Because you're afraid that I'll turn out to be like your husband?"

She felt the panic build, constricting her chest, her ability to get enough air. "What do you know about my husband?"

"Zach let it slip that he wasn't a nice man."

Oh, God. What had her son told him? "I don't want to talk about this, Brandon. It's over now." She walked out, trying to get away from the questions, from having to make up more lies.

It didn't work as Brandon followed her into the small living room.

"Nora, I understand what you're going through."

She swung around. Suddenly she couldn't hold it in

any longer. "No, you don't. You have no idea what it's like to be afraid every day you wake up and wonder what you're going to do to set him off." She clamped her mouth shut, but too late, she'd already revealed too much. When Brandon came toward her, she wanted nothing more than to let him comfort her, to lean into his strength and forget all about the past. Instead she automatically backed up.

"I do know, Nora, because I spent seven years living with an abusive man."

She gasped, and her gaze searched his. "Your dad?"

"No, my mother's first husband. Cade Randell didn't come into my life until I was about Zach's age. That's when he learned I was his biological son."

She watched him, thinking about Abby Randell, recalling her strength, her poise and confidence. "Is that why your mother helped build the shelter?"

Brandon nodded. "The project helped her deal with the past, too. She's helped a lot of women over the years. One of them is my aunt Maura. She came to the shelter with her kids, Jeff and Holly. They'd been on the run from her ex-husband. In fact, they were living in Uncle Wyatt's house when he bought the place. Surprise, you get a house, and a family is included."

Nora didn't want to think about the similarities. "Did her ex-husband ever find her?"

Brandon's gaze hardened. "Yeah, he found out where she was, but Dad and my uncle were waiting. Her ex went to prison, and Wyatt married Maura." He smiled. "And I got two more cousins—Holly is away at college, and Jeff chose a career in the military. They won't be at the rodeo, but you'll get to meet a lot of other cousins."

She shook her head. "No, I can't meet any more of your family." She just realized how sad that made her feel. "They'll think we're together…a couple."

"Is that so bad?"

It would be wonderful, she wanted to shout. But she'd never be free to have a real life. "I don't want to get Zach's hopes up."

Brandon felt Nora was holding something back. "You know and I know, Nora, outside of school Zach doesn't get to interact with anyone but you and Millie. He needs to be around other kids."

"He's only seven. He's too young to go outside by himself. Besides, I have to work."

"Then let him come with me tomorrow. I can take him out to the ranch." He saw her tense. "I won't take him riding, but I'd like to show him around—by Jeep." He raised an eyebrow. "Would you trust me enough to do that?"

She hesitated. "I trust you, Brandon, but there's more to this than a day on the ranch. I know you want more from me than just being my son's babysitter. And I can't give it to you."

He held up a hand. "Friendship, Nora. Can you agree to a friendship? No pressure. I'm watching Zach because you need help. I'm taking him out to the ranch because I need to brush up on some calf roping skills. I thought he'd enjoy it, but if you'd rather have him here…"

She looked thoughtful. "You really mean it about no pressure?"

He nodded, feeling a spark of hope. Maybe he was winning her over. "I swear, Nora. I won't make a move on you. No touching, no hugging, no kissing. We'll just be friends."

This time she folded her arms over her chest and fought a smile. "I'm supposed to believe you."

He acted hurt by her comment. "Please, I'm a sworn officer of the law. When I say I will not make a move on you, I mean it. In fact, if there's going to be any fraternization it'll have to come from you."

Her pretty eyes narrowed. "There won't be."

Brandon leaned forward, leaving mere inches between them. "Think about it, Nora. No more kisses. Kisses where you can't get close enough, you can't taste enough of each other, and feeling as if you'll die if you can't get into each other's skin."

He heard the catch in her breath, watched her eyes darken, but he didn't stop the torment for the both of them. His own body stirred with need and he struggled with his breathing.

"It's not going to be easy for me, either. I've never tasted anyone as sweet as you." His voice grew hoarse with every word. "Talk about a rush. Since the first time I saw you, I can't get you out of my head. At night, I dream of those rich blue eyes of yours." His gaze lowered. "And, oh God, your perfect mouth." He groaned, closed his eyes momentarily, working to gather it together.

"But if you want to be friends…" He shrugged as he took a step back. "Just remember the next time we kiss, you'll be the one who initiates it." He nodded. "I can live with that," he lied as boldly as if his life depended on it. He had to win Nora's trust, and even though this was killing him, he'd do whatever it took.

CHAPTER SEVEN

THE following weekend, Nora drove out to the Circle B Ranch with a chatty Zach in the backseat, announcing all his plans for his day at the rodeo. Since Brandon had brought her son to the ranch just days before, he hadn't talked about anything else.

Nora wasn't going to come today, but Brandon had already invited Zach, so she didn't have any choice unless she wanted to be labeled the meanest mom in the world. There were so many things Zach had already missed in his short life, so she didn't want to keep him from this experience.

Good excuse, girl, she told herself. It had nothing to do with the fact that she, too, wanted to see Brandon today. It had been a long five days since he'd walked out of her apartment, but not before he'd announced she had to make the next move if they were to have a relationship. Coming today, she was not only encouraging her son, but also giving Brandon encouragement that they could possibly have a chance.

This was a bad idea all around.

She'd give anything to be with this man, to live a normal life without the threat of her past intruding. But she couldn't.

"Mom, look," Zach called.

There were rows of multicolored streamers hanging along the fence, and a big banner over the archway, reading, Circle B Annual Rodeo Everyone Welcome.

A tingle of excitement raced through her as she drove though the gate. She was going to see Brandon. She shook off the thought and concentrated on the guy directing them to park in an open field. They got out of the car and walked with the others heading toward the barn and corral. They passed several concession stands that offered a variety of food and drinks. Although they arrived early, there were a lot of people milling around, setting up tables and bleachers for the rodeo.

"Look, Mom, that's where Brandon's going to do the team roping event." The boy looked around, frowning. "He said he was going to meet us."

"Remember, he's on the roundup."

Zach couldn't hide his disappointment. "Oh, I wish I could go with him."

Before Nora could console her son, someone called to them. A smiling Abby approached, dressed in black jeans, a beautiful royal blue Western blouse, topped off with a black cowboy hat.

"Good, you made it," she said. "Hi, Zach, you ready for the big day?"

He nodded. "I just wish Brandon was here."

Abby smiled. "Let's see what I can do about that."

She pulled a slim phone from her hip pocket and punched in a number, then turned to Zach. "The men are driving the cattle in now." Abby paused and spoke into the phone. "They're here. Okay, I will." She hung up, then motioned them to go with her. "Come on, all the action will be in the branding pens. Brandon is out with the herd, but he wanted to know when you got here."

Once they reached the large group of pens, Nora noticed groups of women already camped out. The young and pretty groups were dressed in their best Western gear, tight jeans, boots and fitted blouses.

Suddenly she felt a little frumpy in her own faded jeans and tennis shoes. She had splurged on a Western-cut blouse when she bought Zach a new shirt and jeans for the occasion.

"Look, Mom, here comes Brandon. He's riding really fast."

Nora glanced at the other side of the pens, seeing a man racing toward them on horseback. Her heart skipped a beat at the sight of Brandon on the powerful black stallion. She heard cheers from the rest of the ladies.

Several called his name, and he acknowledged them with a tip of the hat. Then he turned toward her. A big smile crossed his handsome face as he walked his horse to the side of the pen.

"Hi, partner," he called to Zach as he leaned an elbow on the saddle horn.

"Hi, Brandon," her son said.

Brandon turned his attention to her and winked. "Hello, Nora. Glad you could make it."

She struggled for a breath. "Thanks for inviting us."

"Anytime."

Brandon couldn't take his eyes off Nora. The contrast of her startling blue eyes and rich brown hair was breathtaking. "You're always welcome." He glanced back at Zach. "Are you set to go?"

"I have to ask Mom first."

Nora looked puzzled. "What are you talking about?"

Brandon frowned. "Zach was supposed to ask you if he could ride back with me and help bring in the herd."

"Oh, Zach. You're too young."

About that time Abby showed up with the pair of boots Zach had worn on their first visit, but she carried a new hat. The one Brandon had bought for the boy.

"Mom, all the kids get to ride. Brandon's going to watch me." He gave her a pleading look then he slipped on the boots and stood. "Please. I'll never ask for anything again. I promise."

Brandon could see the pained look on Nora's face. She glanced up at him on the big horse.

"Nora, we're not going far. You can see the dust from the herd. We'll be back in about twenty minutes."

She hesitated, but finally relented. "Okay, but be careful."

Brandon grinned, then pointed toward his mom. "Hey, don't forget this."

Abby handed the new straw hat to Zach. "Here, we thought that you needed your own."

"Wow, thanks, Brandon."

"Well, try it on to see if it fits."

Zach did as directed and grinned with his new hat on, then he hurried through the fence gate and to his ride. Brandon reached down and pulled Zach up into the saddle in front of him.

Nora's chest tightened at her son's bright smile as he sat in the saddle in front of Brandon. Brandon then gave the reins to her son. Zach made the clicking sound, then wheeled the horse around. Together they rode off.

She had a feeling that her son had been practicing his riding. He looked too at ease for a raw beginner.

"I know it's hard to let go, Nora," Abby began. "But Brandon will take care of him."

"It's just he's so young and I worry."

Abby watched the riders disappearing in the distance. "I was five when my dad took me out the first time. Of course, my mother nearly skinned him alive. Here in Texas, it's like a rite of passage, especially for boys." Her voice lowered. "And we both know Brandon would never let anything happen to that precious boy. He cares about the both of you too much."

Nora glanced away. She didn't need to hear this. She didn't want to dream about what could happen between them. But this wasn't a dream. It was real life. And for her there wasn't going to be any happy ending.

Brandon was enjoying this roundup more than he had in a long time. Teaching Zach about cattle, and answering his many questions about growing up on a ranch helped put things into perspective.

They were nearly back when he started searching for

Nora. He'd been foolish enough to make that promise about no kissing, and he had no choice but to honor it. But she was here today. That had to be a good sign.

"There's one, Brandon," Zach called, bringing Brandon out of his reverie.

"Let's get him." He dug his heels into Shadow's side and they shot off after the stray calf. Zach was steady in the seat, but Brandon made sure there wasn't any way he could fall off, especially being on a cutting horse with quick moves.

Once the horse had the small animal cornered, Zach waved the lasso and the bawling calf raced off toward the rest of the herd.

"We work pretty good together," Brandon said, suddenly remembering when his dad had taken him out the first time. Although Zach wasn't his son, he felt close to the boy. And his mother, too.

"This is fun," Zach said. "The most fun ever."

"Yeah, this ranks right up there."

They stayed vigilant until the herd approached the pens and were greeted by loud cheers from the gathering crowd.

All Brandon cared about was seeing one person; Nora. He searched the group and found her standing with Hank and Ella. They smiled and waved.

"Hey, Brand, pay attention," Jay yelled at him.

Brandon turned back in time and quickly blocked the path of two strays running out of the chute. "I guess I'm a little rusty."

His brother closed the gate. "I know how to fix that. Spend some time at the ranch."

All at once Brandon was reminded of the family meeting late afternoon, and his decision about the ranch operation.

"We'll discuss it later," he told his brother, then walked Shadow away from the pens.

His thoughts turned to Nora and Zach. What would she think about living out here? He knew Zach would love it here. A ranch was a great place for kids…a family.

Whoa, he was getting ahead of himself. First of all he had to find a way to kiss her. There had to be a way around that one. Right now, he'd take what he could get, spending some time with the mom and her son.

Once he dismounted, he helped Zach down, then handed the animal to one of the ranch hands. They headed toward Nora.

"Mom, did you see me?" Zach called. "We chased that calf back to the herd."

"I saw. You were good."

"Hank, did you see us, too?"

The older man dipped his head. "I sure did, son. I'd say we got us the makings of a cowboy here." Hank turned to his wife and made the introductions.

"It's very nice to meet you," Ella said. "The kids around here call me Grandma Ella."

Although Hank or Ella weren't blood, they'd stepped in to help raise Cade, Chance and Travis when no one else would take them.

Brandon heard Jay call to him. He turned around, knowing that his brother wanted help with the branding. "It looks like I'm not done." He looked at Nora. "I was hoping you'd hang around until I finish. I wanted to take you out to see Mustang Valley."

She shook her head. "You don't need to take me out there. Besides, you have so many things to do today."

"Yes, Nora, you need to go," Hank said. "It's too pretty a place to pass up." He looked at his grandson. "Brandon, you take this lovely girl out there now. I'll find someone to fill in for you." Hank glanced around, searching. "There's got to be someone who wants to show off for all these pretty cowgirls."

Twenty minutes later, Nora sat beside Brandon in the Jeep. She counted her blessings that she wasn't atop a horse. Due to lack of time, and all the activities of the day, Brandon decided to drive her out to the valley.

With Abby's and Ella's insistence, she'd left Zach in their care, but not until she checked his blood sugar levels and made sure he'd eaten. Abby had promised that she wouldn't leave him. Nora had to admit that she was more afraid of being alone with Brandon than of Zach having problems with his insulin.

Brandon turned off the highway onto a gravel road. About half a mile further on, they came to a clearing where he parked at the edge of a rise.

"There aren't any vehicles allowed past this point, so we have to walk the rest of the way. Is that okay for you?"

"Only if my tennis shoes will hold up."

Brandon tipped his hat back and grinned at her. "Guess we're going to have to take some of the city out of the girl and get you some boots." His gaze moved over her body. "You'd look mighty cute in a pair of Western jeans."

Nora started to deny she needed anything, but was distracted seeing the heated look in his eyes. By the time she regained some composure, he climbed out. When he opened her door, she stepped out and was suddenly speechless as she stared at the incredible scenery.

From the ridge she could look down at the lush, grassy meadow. Rows of huge oaks lined a winding rocky bottom creek. The leaves were just starting to change color, in an array of gold and red hues.

Brandon stepped up behind her. "Besides disturbing the mustangs, there aren't any vehicles beyond this point because we rent our cabins to people who prefer quiet and solitude."

She looked around and spotted the nearly hidden cabins scattered along the hillside. Brandon took her hand and led her to stone steps down the ridge. When they reached the bottom, he didn't relinquish his tight grip on her.

"Welcome to Mustang Valley Nature Retreat. You get a better view if you come in on horseback, but we didn't have the time today." He glanced at her. "Next time we won't have to rush."

"Brandon, I probably won't have a chance to come out here again."

Brandon ignored her statement. He wasn't going to give up on her. He was going to concentrate on enjoying being together today. He wanted her to see the special part of this valley. The mustangs.

"Come on." He led her toward one of the large trees, which helped to shield their presence. Brandon stood behind her and pointed toward the meadow where a herd of five ponies wandered toward the creek.

"Oh, Brandon," she whispered.

He felt a shiver run down his spine at her closeness, and forced himself to turn his attention back to the scene. "See that buckskin mare?" His voice was low. "She's been around since I was a kid. That mud-brown and spotted one I don't recognize. It's nice to see they're all in good shape. Of course, Hank makes sure the animals stay healthy. He has a lot of help from our aunt Lindsey. She's the resident vet."

Nora gave him a sideways glance. "Keeping it in the family, huh?"

Seeing the wonder in her eyes, Brandon could only nod. She turned back around to watch the herd and he inhaled her soft scent, causing his gut to tighten.

This isn't the time to think about how much you want this woman, he told himself and fought to keep from touching her. He concentrated on the group of ponies drinking from the creek. Soon a young colt began to run through the high grass.

"Oh, they're precious."

He smiled. "In a way they are. They're part of our country's history. Some people want to destroy them. Others, like Hank, want to keep them safe."

"He's done a wonderful job of it," she said in awe. "He even found them a home. You have to be so proud to be a part of this." Again, she looked at him. "And so lucky to be part of a family that has roots, a home." Her eyes glistened with tears as she quickly glanced away. "We should go back."

He wanted to argue, but stopped himself. From what he knew about her past, she didn't trust easily. He wasn't about to cause her any more stress.

She pushed away from the tree and started up the slope, but the soft wet ground was slippery. With a gasp, she lost her balance and started to fall. Brandon reached her as her knees hit the mud.

He managed to help her stand, then examined the mud on her once white shoes as he pulled out a handkerchief from his pocket. "Like I said, we have to get you some boots for the next time."

She wiped her hands. "I don't need any boots, because I can't come back here again. I came to the rodeo today because of Zach."

The only sound disturbing the silence was the running water in the creek. Luckily it covered the sound of his pounding heart. "I don't believe you, Nora. You're using your son as an excuse for what's happening between us. How can I convince you that I'm not going to hurt you? I care about you and Zach."

Nora couldn't handle his admission. Not now. She had to get away from the temptation, but she couldn't seem to move when Brandon walked to her, or when his hand cupped her chin, making her look at him.

"Nora, you haven't even given us a chance."

His coffee-colored gaze locked on hers, causing a mix of emotions. Her knees grew weak, her breathing labored. All the symptoms of a physical reaction, but she knew it was so much more with this man. She'd never met a man like Brandon Randell.

"Please, Brandon, this wouldn't work between us."

"Tell me why, Nora." He paused. "Is it because of what happened with your husband?"

She shook her head, lying again. She didn't want Jimmy in this. "No, and I don't want to talk about him." She started for the steps, but this time he stopped her.

"Okay, Nora, I won't ask you any more questions about your marriage or your past. I only want you to know that I'm here for you."

"I know," she choked out. She wanted so much to let go. To let Brandon take away all her pain, to give her hope. "I'm afraid." All at once she crumbled and his arms came around her, pulling her against him.

"I'm here, Nora. I'll always be here." He rested his head against her hair, wrapped his arms around her and held her tightly. "I promise, Nora, it's going to be okay."

He drew back and looked at her. "Do you believe me?"

She wanted to so much. She looked up at his handsome face, those piercing dark eyes. God help her, she didn't want to walk away. "Can we just take this slow?"

"I'll take it moment to moment if that helps."

"Could we just enjoy today?"

"Sounds good to me." He gave a half smile. "How about we seal the deal with a kiss?"

Nora knew he was asking her to reach out to him. She also knew once this got started there was no turning back. She rose up on her toes, and wrapped her arms around his neck. Brandon was offering everything she'd ever wanted, even if it was just for a day.

On the way back, they'd detoured by Brandon's parents' house, after he'd called to ask if Nora could borrow a pair of boots and clean jeans. Abby told her to take whatever she needed. After picking out the clothes, they were back at the rodeo in time for lunch.

In the dining hall Nora saw Zach was doing well, so she went in search of Brandon's mother to thank her for the loan of the outfit.

Abby smiled. "I'm glad they fit you so well." She examined the jeans more closely. "In fact, it's a shame you've been hiding that nice figure of yours."

Nora realized that Brandon had noticed, too. He hadn't been able to take his eyes off of her since she'd changed into the fitted jeans. Okay, so she liked the attention.

Brandon stayed close and ate lunch with her and Zach, who monopolized the conversation by talking about all the friends he'd made. Of course, nothing was going to stop him from seeing Brandon in the rodeo.

When Zach carried their empty plates to the trash, Brandon leaned toward Nora. "Are you going to watch me, too?"

She couldn't help but smile. "Of course, it's my chance to watch a real cowboy in action. I wouldn't miss it."

He sighed. "You might be disappointed—I'm pretty rusty."

She felt another rush go through her. "Not a chance."

His gaze darkened and he groaned. "You don't know

how badly I want to kiss you right now." Suddenly they realized from the many sounds of the crowded hall they weren't alone. "I wish we were still out at Mustang Valley."

So did she. "It's a beautiful place." Memories of their visit would always stay with her.

"My parents seem to think so. I've heard rumors that I was conceived there."

Heat rushed to Nora's face as her eyes widened. "You made that up."

He grinned, causing tiny lines around his eyes. "No, I'm not. Of course, back then there weren't any cabins or roads to get there. They were pretty young, and since my grandfather Moreau hated the idea of his daughter associating with a bad Randell boy, they had no other place to go for privacy. In the valley, they only had the wild mustangs to share it with." His gaze moved over her face, stopping at her mouth. "A pretty…stimulating combination, I'd say."

Brandon shifted on the bench seat, trying to ease his discomfort. Served him right. He was crazy for trying to seduce Nora with all these people around. Of course, he did enjoy seeing the passion in her eyes. He was falling hard for this woman.

All at once he felt a hand on his back and his uncle's voice. "Hey, Brand, I hate to break this up. But we have an event to win." Travis Randell smiled at Nora. "Hi, Nora."

"Hi, Travis," she returned. Brandon's uncle was yet another good-looking Randell man with that familiar cleft chin and piercing brown eyes. My goodness, there wasn't a plain one in the bunch.

"So you came to see your fella in the rodeo?"

"Actually Brandon was kind enough to invite Zach. He's the big rodeo fan."

A big smile transformed Travis's face. "Maybe after you watch Brandon today, you'll become one, too." He tipped his hat. "Come on, nephew, it's time to get to work," he said, and walked off.

Brandon started to get up, but Nora reached for him. Before she could think about what she was doing. She leaned forward and kissed him. When Brandon cupped her cheeks, she moaned and he deepened the kiss. Finally he pulled away, his eyes dark and searching.

Somehow she managed to speak. "Just so you know, I'm a big fan, too."

Two hours later, Nora sat in the stands along with Zach, enjoying the rodeo. Several Randells had participated, and most made it into the final round, including Brandon in the team roping event.

Nora told herself that she'd done everything to discourage the man, but he kept coming back. It wasn't fair to him to lead him on, but she couldn't seem to stop herself. Just this once she wanted to stop worrying about her troubles. But she knew better.

She closed her eyes and saw Jimmy's smirking face, telling her she'd never be free of him. That she'd die before he ever let her go. A shiver raced through her and her eyes shot open.

"Mom, Brandon's next to calf rope," Zach called to her. Nora looked down to the arena where Brandon was waving at them. She also heard several other women screaming his name. Why not? He was the kind of man who drew women. She glanced around the crowded bleachers and something caught her attention.

There was a large man sitting alone. He had on the standard cowboy hat and jeans, but he didn't seem to fit in. He wore dark glasses, and she had an odd feeling his gaze was settled on her. She shivered and quickly glanced away. Once again she thought about Jimmy sending someone to find her, but brushed it aside. Brandon had caught the man who attacked her. Pete Carlson.

Was she just being paranoid? Or was someone after her? She knew what she had to do if that happened. That meant she needed to change locations again. She and Zach had to leave town.

She touched her mouth, reliving Brandon's kiss. She didn't want to give him up just yet. She wanted today for both her and Zach.

And maybe, for a little while, they both could dream about ranches and rodeos and one special cowboy.

CHAPTER EIGHT

BRANDON stood behind the chute. He held Shadow's reins, trying to calm his nerves. Limited practice time had only given him a couple days with Travis to hone his roping skills. He did enjoy hanging out with his uncle, and was glad he got to compete today.

The first round had gone pretty well, but he'd only caught one of the calf's legs and it had cost them points. Yet somehow, the uncle/nephew team roping combo still made the finals.

When the announcer called their names, he climbed on his horse.

"Come, son," Travis said. "Let's go do it again. For Randell pride."

Brandon sat a little straighter in the saddle. "For Randell pride," he answered back.

His uncle grinned, then took the header position behind the gate on his roan gelding. Brandon had the healer position on Shadow. All he had to do was rope both hind legs this time, and they'd be home free.

As soon as the horn went off, Travis shot off after the calf, swinging his lasso over his head. Brandon was close behind. With a quick flip, Travis captured the steer, jerking him to a stop. Then it was Brandon's turn. It all came back to him as he went to work and hit his target, then backed Shadow up, making the ropes taut. The judge's flag dropped and the crowd cheered. Brandon looked down at the stretched out calf. Both hind legs were caught in the rope.

He smiled at his work, then it turned to a big grin when he heard their time. They'd won the event. He accepted a high-five from Travis, and then searched the stands for Nora.

He finally found her and Zach in the overflowing crowd toward the top of the bleachers. His chest puffed out a little when he saw her eager wave.

Travis shifted in his saddle. "Good job, Brand." He glanced up in the stands, too. "Seems there's a pretty lady wanting to congratulate you."

"Yeah, it's kind of nice," Brandon said, then heard Travis's name called. He turned to see Aunt Josie. The petite brunette stood by the gate waving and cheering. "Seems someone is pretty happy with you, too."

Travis looked at his wife of over twenty-five years. There was no denying the love, showing on the rancher's face. Brandon wanted that. That same love as his parents, and his uncles had. Hopefully one day…

"Let's go get our prize," Travis said. "I got a lady to kiss."

They picked up their buckles and ribbons from the

announcer and rode out of the arena into the holding area. His uncle found Josie and claimed his kiss.

Brandon heard his name being called and turned in time as Zach launched his small body in his direction, and he caught the boy in midflight.

"You won," Zach cried. "I knew you would 'cause you're the best cowboy."

Brandon felt a sudden tightness around his heart. "I don't know about that," he said. "But today, we were good enough to be first." He handed the boy the buckle and ribbon. "Here, these are for you."

Zach's eyes lit up. "I get to keep them?"

"Sure." Brandon set Zach down, then turned to a smiling Nora. His gaze locked with her blue eyes and he was unable to look away.

"I got to show these to Buddy," Zach said. "Can I, Mom?"

She didn't move her gaze from Brandon. "Stay close by," she warned.

The boy took off and Brandon stepped closer to her. "How about you, Nora, do you think I'm the best cowboy?"

She nodded. "You are for me."

Two hours later, with the rodeo over and the barbecue starting up outside, Brandon sat at Hank and Ella's dining room table. His mother and father were at the head, with his brother, Jay, and sister, Kristin, across from him on the other side. Talk about feeling alone.

"Should I have brought my lawyer for this business meeting?" Brandon joked.

His father frowned. "At least that tells me you've been thinking about resolving this."

That had been the only thing he'd spent his time thinking about. Suddenly Nora came to mind. Well, not all his time…

"Maybe."

His dad didn't look happy. "You know, I'm really tired of this…"

Abby placed her hand on her husband's arm. "Son, why don't you tell us what you've decided?"

Brandon glanced at Jay and Kristin. "I know I haven't been very active in ranch business lately."

"No lie," Jay huffed.

He glared at his brother. "And you've gotten paid well for running things."

"But I'm working your ranch."

Brandon nodded in agreement, then turned to his young sister. She looked like their mother with her auburn hair and green eyes. And just as pretty. He was sad he hadn't spent much time with her lately, and a little ashamed he didn't know what her plans were for the future. "Kristin, are you planning to come back here, I mean after college?"

"Of course." She smiled. "I want to teach in the area. But I also want to stay involved in the business."

"That's just it," Brandon said. "Randell Corporation isn't a small business anymore. All six connecting ranches need to contribute to make it successful."

Always the financial advisor, his father said, "And

because everyone contributes the corporation is doing well."

"Lately I haven't been doing my share toward that success, and I don't know how much I'll be able to in the future."

"You've been building your career," his mother said.

But it wasn't ranching, he thought. And this was a ranch.

Brandon released a sigh and looked at Jay and Kristin. "I was the only grandchild when Grandpa Moreau was alive. He taught me to ride a horse. He bought me my first hat." He glanced at his mother and saw her smile over the memories. There were bad memories, too. Tom Moreau hated the Randells, and did everything he could to keep Brandon from his real dad. Let it go, he told himself.

"I also know that if you two had been born then, Grandpa would have divided the ranch equally between all of us. I think the only fair thing to do is share ownership."

Jay grinned and so did Kristin.

"There's one exception, though. When you and Mom decide the house is too big, I'd like to have it."

That brought a grin to his parents' faces and they exchanged a glance. "How about in about six months?" his mother said.

"No, please, you don't have to leave so soon."

His father held up a hand. "We've already been planning to move, Brandon. Hank gave us land years ago. We've already picked out a sweet spot with a great view of the valley, and soon, we'll be breaking ground for our dream home." Cade Randell reached for his wife's hand.

Brandon knew years ago Hank had divided sections of the Circle B Ranch between the brothers, and Hank's biological daughter, Josie. "Mom, Dad…are you sure about this?"

His parents smiled at each other, then turned toward their children. His mother couldn't hide the emotion in her eyes. "It's time. It's time for the next generation."

While Brandon had been taking care of his family business, Nora had gone to the car to retrieve her and Zach's clothes for the evening's festivities. She had changed into a gauzy black skirt, an eggshell-colored peasant blouse and a pair of sandals, borrowing a long silver chain necklace and a rope belt from Millie. Satisfied with her looks, Nora went in search of Zach.

In the bathroom in the dining hall, Nora cleaned the day's grime off her son and had him change into clean clothes. She also tested his blood sugar and administered his shot before he went back to eat with the other kids. Nora strolled outside to the patio area where she had agreed to meet Brandon.

Happy with yet another successful rodeo, Hank wandered through the crowds greeting old friends and new ones, when he spotted Nora. Not only was she an attractive woman, but he liked her a lot. More importantly, so did his grandson.

"Well, you look mighty pretty tonight."

Nora smiled at him. "Thank you. And thank you for today, Hank. Zach and I are having a great time."

"I'm glad. You and your son are always welcome here." He arched an eyebrow. "I'm sure Brandon will bring you back again."

She hesitated, then nodded. "That would be nice."

Hank took hold of her hand. "It's not because he's my grandson that I say this, but he's a fine young man."

"I know, and he's been wonderful to me and Zach. He's been working so hard to help me with all the trouble I had."

"I doubt Brandon thinks of you as a job."

She released a long breath. "I'm not sure I'll be staying in the area."

Hank frowned. "Oh, that's a shame. I had a feeling you and that fine boy of yours were fitting in here."

She swallowed. "Sometimes there isn't a choice."

Hank Barrett studied her. "And sometimes running is not the best thing, either. I've found out that it eventually catches up with you. Maybe if you meet the problem head-on then things can be worked out."

He saw her tense. "Not this time."

He wanted to push for more information, but knew better. "If you need help, I want you to know we're here." Then he pulled her into a tight hug and whispered, "Just remember, Nora Donnelly, you don't have to be blood to be part of this family."

She held on. "Thank you," she managed to say.

Hank pulled back and gave her a wink. "I better go. I don't think I want to tangle with that young cowboy."

Nora turned around and saw Brandon walking toward them. In a pair of blue jeans and a black Western shirt, he tossed them an easy grin. "Hey, Granddad, you tryin' to steal my gal?"

"Tryin' is about all I'm doing." Hank placed Nora's hand into Brandon's. "She's all yours." He turned and walked off.

Brandon couldn't take his eyes off Nora. "You look pretty."

She smiled shyly. "So do you," she said. "I mean you look handsome."

"Maybe we should go get something to eat. I'm starved for some of that delicious Circle B beef."

Together they walked toward the patio area. Strings of lights were hung from tree to tree and soft music filled the background.

"How did your meeting go?" she asked.

"Well, as soon as I sign the papers, I'll only own a third of a ranch."

She cocked her head. "Is that what you want?"

"Yeah. It's the way it should have been a long time ago." He filled her in on some of details earlier. "It was the only fair thing to do. Jay wants to continue with the day-to-day operations, and run his own herd. Kristin is still in college, but I want her to have a home here always."

She gave him a sideways glance. "You are so lucky to have a big family."

He stopped and wanted so badly to kiss her. "I know. And I'm seriously thinking about moving back here. My parents want to retire, and have their heart set on building a place in the valley." He looked at her. "So the ranch house is mine. Only problem is it's too big for one person. Got any ideas on how I should fill it?"

The night was a great cap to a near perfect day, and Brandon had loved sharing it with Nora; the trip to Mustang Valley, going on the roundup with Zach, winning the team roping event. And the evening was looking promising as he held her in his arms and they moved around the makeshift dance floor to a Country-Western ballad.

Since he was a kid, he'd been to a lot of these rodeos, brought girls, too, but this was by far the best time. Nora was different. And Zach. Who would have thought he'd be crazy about a seven-year-old kid? But he was Nora's kid. And Brandon wanted them both in his life. He'd realized that today when he'd told his parents he wanted to live in the house and also get closer to the family.

He might continue to work for the sheriff's office, but he couldn't erase his roots here any more than he could move out of Texas.

Now, all he had to do was convince Nora to stay in San Angelo and give their relationship a chance. Hopefully to start a life together. The music ended and he slowly pulled back, but didn't release her. "That was nice."

She nodded. "It's been a long time since I've danced. I'm not very good."

He didn't know much about her first marriage, only that her first husband was not a good man. "I wasn't thinking about the steps, only how you felt in my arms with your body pressed against mine. I could get used to this."

He could see the heat in her gaze. "Oh, Brandon. I thought we were going to take it a day at a time?"

He didn't want to hear her doubts. "Then I guess we shouldn't waste any of it." He wanted privacy while he stated his case as to why they should stay together. Taking her hand, he walked her off the dance floor, through the crowd of people and past the numerous tables. He picked up his pace on the gravel driveway, along the white-slatted fence and away from the noise and festivities so he could convince her of his feelings.

With the combination of soft music in the background and the dim light to protect them, he only wanted to kiss away her doubts.

"I want more than just today, Nora. I want tomorrow, too, and the next day."

Nora ached with the same need. God help her, she wanted a chance with Brandon. "I'm no good at this. My marriage was a disaster. I'm afraid—"

"I'm not your husband. I'd never intentionally hurt you, Nora," he promised. "I'm crazy about you and Zach." He stepped closer and gripped her shoulders. She was trembling, or was it him? "Just give it a chance, Nora. For us." He lowered his head and brushed his mouth against hers. She gasped but couldn't make herself pull away. He went back again and again and her arms slipped around his neck as she rose up to meet his kiss.

His mouth opened over hers and she pulled tight against him. Her heart was drumming in her chest as his tongue danced with hers. He swallowed her soft whimper and deepened the kiss, angling his mouth over hers, trying to get closer.

He finally came up for air and rested his forehead against hers. "I want you. Tonight."

"Brandon," she breathed.

He smiled. "I like you saying my name. Say it again."

She hesitated, then rushed out with, "Brandon…"

Brandon's covered her mouth once again as his hands moved over her back and lower, clutching the fabric of her skirt, drawing her against him. He released her mouth, and rained kisses over her face and neck. This time she moaned and cupped his face, kissing him, pressing herself further into him.

The entire world was slowly fading away when suddenly there was a burst of applause in the background, letting them know how close they were to losing it, and how fleeting their privacy was. It became a reality when they heard Zach calling their names.

They broke apart in time to see the seven-year-old running toward them. Brandon reached out and caught him. "Whoa, partner. What got you in such a hurry?"

Those wide eyes shone even in the dim light. "I won. I really won."

"What did you win?" Brandon asked.

The boy swallowed. "The horse. I won the horse at the raffle."

Nora frowned. "How could you win a horse, Zach?"

Brandon froze, then finally said, "Ah, I might have bought a ticket and put Zach's name on it."

Zach's eyes widened as he nodded. "Yeah, Mom. Hawk's Flame is my horse now."

Within the hour Nora had packed up her and Zach's belongings, and after some long goodbyes they'd headed toward the car. The ownership of the horse would have to be dealt with later. Even though Brandon had offered Zach to leave it at the ranch, Nora couldn't ask him to board an animal she couldn't afford to keep in the first place. Besides, she and Zach would be leaving San Angelo, and probably Texas. Soon.

She didn't have any choice. If Jimmy found out she was here, there wasn't any telling what he'd do. It would be safer for everyone to move on. Maybe east. Florida, or South Carolina, or Georgia. All she knew was she needed to get lost in the crowd again.

Her thoughts turned to Brandon. She tried not to lead him on, but that was exactly what she'd done. And she wasn't going to end it yet. If he wanted to stay tonight, she wouldn't turn him away. She had made the mistake of getting close to someone, and so had Zach. It would cost them both.

She glanced in the backseat and saw her sleeping son. She smiled. He'd had a near perfect day. At least she'd been able to give him that before they had to leave town. No matter what it cost them both, she wanted some sort of normalcy for her son. And for herself, she needed to know what it was like to be with a man who cared about her and her feelings, her needs. She didn't want it to go beyond the physical desire with Brandon, but it had and that meant it would be harder to walk away.

Nora turned off the highway and drove toward her complex, then pulled into her spot and Brandon parked next to her. She shook her son awake. "Zach, wake up. We're home."

Before she could get her son motivated, Brandon opened the back door. "Let him sleep…I'll carry him inside."

He looked at Nora. Her heart began to race, knowing he was giving her the choice as to whether he stayed tonight. Good Lord, she couldn't turn him down.

"Thank you, I'd like that."

Brandon smiled. "My pleasure, ma'am," he told her as he unfastened the seat belt and lifted the boy into his arms.

Zach mumbled a few words and opened his eyes and smiled. "Are we home?"

Brandon smiled back at the boy, hoping he wouldn't wake up too much. He had plans tonight and that didn't include a third party. "Yeah, and in a few minutes you'll be in bed."

The boy yawned and laid his head on Brandon's shoulder. "Will you take me?"

Brandon wanted nothing more. "Sure, but we're going to condense it tonight—pajamas and teeth brushing. It's too late for a story." He wanted all the time he could get with Nora. "If that's okay with your mom."

"Sounds perfect."

Brandon carried his precious cargo toward the steps, thinking how he could get used to this. He glanced at

Nora. Oh, yeah, he most definitely could handle evenings with this woman, and the boy.

"It's been a nice day."

"Yes, it was," she admitted.

It would be hard, but he would do what he promised her, and take things slow. They reached the landing and headed upstairs to her apartment. Suddenly he realized the porch light was out, and further investigation revealed her door was ajar.

The lawman in him went on alert, and he put out an arm stopping Nora from going any further. Silently he directed her back down the steps to the truck. He opened the door and set Zach down on the seat.

"Get in, Nora." He directed her into the passenger side.

She climbed in, looking frightened. "Is there someone inside my apartment?"

"I'm not sure, but I'm not taking any chances." He took out his phone and called for backup, then opened the glove compartment and reached for the weapon he carried in the truck. He tucked the gun into his belt.

Nora grabbed hold of his arm. "Brandon, don't go up there alone. What if they're still there?"

He nodded. "If someone's up there, I can't let them get away. So lock yourselves in and don't leave the truck. No matter what. I'll be back."

She continued to hold on to him. "Please, be careful."

"Always." Brandon squeezed her hand, then closed the door shut. He ran across the small lawn to the steps, taking them two at a time. Gun drawn, he paused and listened beside the partly open door. Not hearing anything, he silently moved inside, keeping his body flat against the wall as he glanced around.

The drapes were closed, but the light over the stove cast a dim shadow over the empty room and the destruction. The place was in shambles; all the furniture had been turned over, drawers in the kitchen emptied onto the floor.

He continued down the hall, careful not to trip on any of the debris. His pulse pounded in his ears as he checked both bedrooms. Seeing there was no one there, he flicked on the light to assess the damage.

Returning to the living room, he saw that everything was either overturned or broken. Even the sofa cushions had been sliced opened. "Damn, this was a personal attack."

Brandon headed outside as a patrol car pulled up. Nora got out of the truck and ran to him. "What happened?"

"Someone did break in. I'm sorry, Nora, the place is a mess. You can check for missing valuables later."

She looked panicked. "But I need to go up there." She stated as she started for the steps, but he stopped her.

"You can't, Nora. It's a crime scene now."

"Zach needs his insulin."

"I'll take you to the hospital to get some more," he promised, then walked off to meet up with Deputy Griggs.

"Any sign of the perpetrator?" the young officer asked.

Brandon shook his head. "They're gone." His cell phone went off and he answered it. "Randell."

"Brandon. Captain Marks. How does it look there?"

"It's not good." He turned away so he could talk to

his commanding officer. "Nora Donnelly's apartment has been broken into and pretty much everything was destroyed. Did Carlson make bail, yet?"

"Yeah, he was just released."

"Then we need to pick him up again."

"Can't do it. Carlson had an alibi for the night Nora Donnelly was attacked," the captain said.

That couldn't be. "So he gets out and comes here to punish his accuser?"

"Hold on a minute." Brandon waited about two minutes and his captain came back. "Randell, I just checked with the jail, Carlson was released not twenty minutes ago. I doubt he could get across town and do the deed without getting caught red-handed."

He glanced at Nora, then walked out of earshot. "Then who did this?"

"You're a detective, Randell. I guess that makes it your job to find evidence, DNA, anything to find out who's been after Mrs. Donnelly. Pete Carlson didn't have anything to do with this attack."

Brandon couldn't believe it. The man was quick tempered, and used his fists on women. "He's the logical suspect."

Brandon heard a sigh. "You're still new at this, Randell, so you'll learn it isn't always about logic. Now, we have to start at the beginning and see if there's something we missed. Talk with Mrs. Donnelly and see if there is anyone else. This all seems too personal to me."

Brandon's head was pounding, not wanting to believe

the proof, or the alternative. He looked at Nora talking with Jason Griggs. She wasn't telling him everything.

Brandon hung up and went to speak with Griggs, letting him know to call him if anything came up. Now, he had to find Nora and Zach a safe place to stay.

He walked back to them. "I think we better find a drugstore and pick up a few essentials."

Zach looked teary-eyed. "Where are we going to live now?"

Brandon ruffled the boy's hair. "How would you like to stay with me for a few days?"

CHAPTER NINE

Two hours later, despite being tucked away safely in Brandon's condo, Nora couldn't stop shaking.

He'd found her. He'd been the one who'd caused her attack in the parking lot, hacked into her bank account and trashed her apartment. It was all Jimmy's doing.

Nora pulled the lapels of the borrowed robe tighter over the extra large T-shirt, trying to stop herself shaking. It didn't work. She glanced around the master suite where her son was sound asleep under the covers in the large bed.

The room was like the man; large and masculine. The furniture was dark, and the comforter navy with tan and brown pillows. The pictures on the dresser were of his family. She glanced at the photo of a teenage Brandon with his horse. Another showed him at his college graduation, standing beside his proud parents. Family and roots—that was what was important to the Randells. And letting Brandon get involved in her life, she'd put them all in harm's way.

Did Jimmy have her followed out to the ranch? Had

someone been watching them? How sick was that? What was worse, she knew her ex-husband wouldn't stop until he had her back in his power.

She went to the window. The blinds were closed, but she sneaked a peek out from the second story down to the deserted street.

Was he out there watching her now? Even from jail, Jimmy had connections. There were too many people on his payroll who would be more than willing to do the job of getting rid of her.

A feeling of doom clouded any optimism she once had of making a decent, safe life for herself and Zach. She glanced at her sleeping son. Her mothering instincts were to do anything she could to save her child. He deserved a chance at life. A normal life.

No, she couldn't let Jimmy take her son. He didn't want Zach anyway. He wanted her. She shut her eyes, thinking of the cruel man she'd married, the man she'd once loved and now hated. She'd never go back, never let him touch her child, ever again. That was why somehow she had to get out of town.

Her thoughts turned to Brandon. As much as he wanted to help, she couldn't let him jeopardize his safety. This time she had to end it. Then she had to leave, and fast.

Brushing a kiss on Zach's forehead, she left the room. In the hall, she walked to the second bedroom that was made into an office. There was a sofa bed against one wall, and a large desk with a computer against the other. That was where Brandon sat, talking on the phone.

Brandon ended the call, frustrated and angry with himself. Although there were no clues on who had broken into Nora's apartment, just as there were no clues as to who attacked her, he'd discovered a lot about the woman he'd fallen for.

He turned toward the doorway and saw her standing there. Even in his too-big bathrobe, she looked pretty. He glanced away. No, he couldn't let his feelings get in the way of this investigation.

He stood. "I'm sorry about the lack of wardrobe. There wasn't much that was salvageable from the apartment."

"I only care that Zach and I are safe."

"It's not okay, Nora," he said as he ran his fingers through his hair. "Someone's after you. He's made two attempts on you and I haven't been able to stop him." He glared at her. "But you haven't been much help, either."

"I've told you everything I know."

He'd wanted her to trust him enough to tell him the truth. "I don't buy that. Dammit, Nora. Both attacks were personal." Too personal to be just random, he added silently.

She blinked at his harsh words.

"I can't help you if you don't tell me everything." He couldn't keep the frustration out of his voice.

She stood there, her throat working nervously. "Don't you think I know that?" She walked to the sofa. "It's not going to matter anyway. It's not going to stop him."

He went to her. "Stop who?"

Before she could say any more, the phone rang. Brandon raised a hand. "We're not finished," he told her.

"Randell," he said into the receiver.

"Brandon, it's Jason. I got a match on the fingerprints from the apartment."

He sat down. "Great, give me the names."

He heard the hesitation in Jason's voice. "We only got one set. It was on Nora Donnelly, but the prints say her name is Kathryn Nora Mullins. She had a juvenile record."

All at once air was trapped in his lungs.

Jason continued. "I investigated further and found a marriage license, but also a divorce decree dated two years ago."

"Who to?"

"A Jimmy Archer. I found him in the system, too. He also has an alias of Rey Alcazar and is in jail right now, awaiting trial in San Diego, California, on drug trafficking charges. Man, this guy's got a rap sheet as long as my arm."

His gaze shot to Nora. "I'll have a look at it later."

"Yeah, I'm sorry, Brandon."

"Nothing to be sorry about." He felt like a fool. "Are there any outstanding warrants on Mrs. Archer?"

Nora's head jerked up.

"No, she's clean."

"Thanks, Jason."

Brandon hung up and looked at Nora, suddenly seeing a stranger. Somehow he had to put aside any feelings for her and do his job. He walked around to the other side of the desk and sat down on the corner. "It's your ex-husband that's after you, isn't it?"

"We don't know it's him." She couldn't look him in the eye. "Besides, he's in jail."

"Why, Nora? What did you do to him to make him angry enough to attack you?"

Her gaze met his, but he didn't like the panic he saw.

A dozen different scenarios raced through his mind. "Okay, answer me this, is it anything illegal?"

She nodded slowly. "I kidnapped my son."

Brandon tried to stay professional, but it was impossible. Too many emotions were tearing him apart. He'd come to care for both Nora and Zach.

"Is that why you didn't tell me who you really are?" he asked.

"I wasn't going to tell a law officer that I kidnapped my son and crossed the state line."

He pushed aside the hurt from her lies, and tried to concentrate on doing his job. "There's no warrant for you. Tell me why your husband didn't report you?"

Nora folded her arms across her chest and stared out the window. "Because Jimmy plays by his own rules. Sending guys to rough me up turns him on."

"You have rights, Nora. You're the one who convinced Karen Carlson to get help."

She looked over her shoulder at him. "This is different. I had no proof of abuse. Besides, Jimmy has money and power, and he used Zach against me. Even after the divorce, I couldn't move out of his house. He found a way to get me fired from jobs so I couldn't support myself. And I needed to make sure that Zach was taken care of and Jimmy used that to his advantage."

Brandon's fists clenched. "Men like your ex are scum."

Nora agreed, but it didn't matter. "I tried to get help, I really did. The only way to make sure Zach was okay was to stay at the house."

Her words sounded pathetic even to her. "And I was doing all right the past few months, until I was attacked in the parking lot." She flinched. "It's Jimmy's way of punishing people when they cross him." She took a shaky breath. "I should have taken off after the night I was attacked. We'd be miles away."

"No, that's the worst thing you could have done. We can protect you."

"What will you do, take me into custody?" Tears flooded her eyes as she bit down on her bottom lip. "Oh, God. Zach. What's going to happen to him if Jimmy gets to me?"

Brandon shook his head as he started to reach for her, but stopped. "Like I said, there isn't a warrant for you. So for now both of you are safe. But you have to trust me, Nora."

Wiping her tears, she nodded. "Okay."

"How did you get away from him?

"When Jimmy got arrested, he wasn't at the house. I didn't even stop to think, I just needed to get Zach out of there and as far away as I could. In the past, Jimmy always managed to get off on a technicality. This time, though, the judge refused him bail because of his import/export business into Mexico. Before the police got a warrant to search the house, I found the combination to Jimmy's wall safe and took some money out, then I took insulin and some clothes, whatever would fit in a small bag, then with Zach we hurried out of the compound and called a taxi."

"How much money did you take?"

She glanced away. "About twenty thousand dollars."

He whistled.

"I didn't take it all. I had to buy a used car, but I only spent what I needed until I found a job. Mostly I used the money for Zach's medicine." She searched Brandon's face for any sign of sympathy. "You've got to let me go."

The pain and fear in her voice tore at Brandon. "Do you really think that your ex-husband will stop coming after you?"

"If he's in jail, I have time to get away. There's plenty of money left, and the evidence I have will keep him away from me, whether he's in jail or not. Please, Brandon, just let—"

"What evidence?"

She glanced away. "There was a small ledger hidden in between one of the bundles of bills. It has names of people and drug transactions."

"Good Lord, Nora. No wonder the man sent people after you. You still have it?"

She nodded.

"Then you need to turn it into the authorities."

"Don't you think I tried? Before leaving San Diego, I was to meet a police detective at a coffee shop. When

I got to the location, I recognized one of Jimmy's men with him. No, the only chance I have is to take Zach and keep going."

"And you'll end up looking over your shoulder for the rest of you life. I don't want to find you and Zach lying dead somewhere."

She gasped. "I wouldn't let that happen."

"Then stay and cooperate with the sheriff and I'll call in the DEA. You might have the key to strengthen the case against Jimmy." He froze, then said, "Where's the ledger?"

"In a safe place."

He studied her for a second or two. "Then you need to decide where to go from here, Nora. Is it Nora, or do I call you Kathryn?"

She shook her head. "No, I'm Nora Donnelly from now on."

He released a breath. "So do I call the sheriff?"

She hesitated, then nodded.

"Okay," he stood.

She placed her hand on his arm to stop him. "I'm scared, Brandon."

"So am I, Nora." His gaze locked with hers. "I'm going to do everything I can to keep you and Zach safe. You have my word."

A few hours later, Brandon hung up the phone after talking to the sheriff, one of many calls they'd exchanged back and forth during the night. Brandon blew out a breath. It wasn't over yet.

The DEA was involved now. It seemed Jimmy

Archer, aka Rey Alcazar, had been under surveillance for suspicion of drug trafficking for a while now. So they were very interested in the ledger Nora had taken from Archer's home.

Earlier, he'd learned from Nora about her journey over the past months. In Arizona, she had found someone willing to get phony IDs for her—for a price. She was a nurse, but had to get her license under her new identity, taking the name "Donnelly" because it was her grandmother's. That might have been how Archer found her. It was good thinking on Nora's part to put the ledger in a locker.

Brandon headed upstairs, knowing from the very beginning how fast and intense things had gotten between Nora and him. She had tried to warn him off, but he hadn't taken the hints. How could he when he had fallen for her the second he'd laid eyes on her? And now, he might just have to back away for good.

Brandon walked down the hall to his bedroom, where he found Zach sound asleep in the bed. His mother was tucked in close behind her son, a protective arm over his slight body.

Brandon had some idea of how scared Zach must have felt living with an animal like Archer, remembering his own stepfather's special form of abuse. No way would he let that man back into Nora and Zach's life.

He studied Nora. She looked so peaceful in sleep, but how many nights had she been too frightened to close her eyes? How many days had she been afraid that she'd be found?

He wished he could take away that fear and all the pain of her past. Careful not to disturb her, he sat down on the edge of the bed. His chest tightened with the overwhelming need to lie down beside her. Just to watch her, hold her for as long as he had her here. To dream of what might have been if things were different. If Nora could stay and give them a chance. If she would let him love her. But he couldn't think about his own feelings now. Their safety had to come first.

Nora moved closer, wanting his touch, aching for his hands on her. She moaned as she rolled onto her back and her eyes shot open to find the room dark. And no Brandon. Just a glimmer of a light coming from the hall.

She lay back on the pillow, trying to recall her now illusive dream, but her thoughts were interrupted when the events of the day came rushing back.

Warm and restless, Nora slipped out of bed, careful not to disturb a sleeping Zach. She grabbed her borrowed robe and walked down the hall. In the office, she found Brandon talking on the phone. He glanced up, but didn't look happy to see her. She couldn't blame him.

"You should try and get some rest," he told her.

Not without you, she wanted to shout. She wanted him to hold her, to comfort her. Now, there was this uneasy distance between them. "You should be in bed, too."

"I have work to do. Besides, considering what you've told me, you'll both need round-the-clock protection."

She went to the sofa and sat down. "I never meant for this to happen. Not to you, or your family."

Brandon stood and stretched his arms over his head, revealing his lengthy torso covered by a fitted black T-shirt, and jeans hanging low on his narrow hips.

Her pulse jumped into double time. She closed her eyes, doubting she'd ever have a peaceful night's sleep again.

He went to her and sat down next to her. "You need to make some decisions."

"I know. After I turn over the ledger, I need to get far away from Jimmy as possible."

His gaze narrowed. "He caught up with you once, he could do it again. You need to make sure he stays in jail. That means cooperate."

"Cooperate! I tried that so many times. Where was law enforcement when I needed them? When I tried to leave and get full custody of my son? No one believed me…no one was there for us. Now, you want me to risk our lives so the government can make a case against Jimmy!"

"I won't let that happen," he argued.

She stood and crossed the room. "What do you care? Since you've learned the truth about me you act as if I have the plague."

He went to her. "Dammit, I have to. It's my job to protect you and Zach. I can't let my personal feelings distract me."

"Well, you're very good at your job, Detective Randell." She started to leave, when he grabbed her arm and swung her around to face him.

His dark gaze was intense, smoldering, but she wasn't frightened. Never of Brandon. Slowly his hold on her relaxed and finally he reached out and he cupped her face with his palm.

Nora's heart was pounding against her ribs; every nerve ending in her body was electrified. She should back away, but that wasn't an option with this man.

He made a groaning sound as he lowered his head until his mouth was only inches from hers. Just then there was a sharp knock at the door.

He released her. "That'll be federal agents—you better get dressed." Then he turned and left her as if nothing had passed between them.

Brandon opened the door to find two men dressed in black trousers, open collared shirts and dark jackets. They held up their badges.

"Detective Randell, I'm Agent Matt Conroy and this is Agent Dan Paulson. We're here to speak with Mrs. Archer."

Brandon checked the IDs then stepped aside. "She'll be down shortly. We didn't expect you so soon." He led them into the kitchen. "Coffee?"

Both men nodded, and Conroy spoke. "This case takes top priority."

They sat down at the counter. "We've been building a case against Archer for two years," Paulson began. "He was born in Mexico as Rey Alcazar. Once in the U.S., he changed it to Archer. And over the years, he's managed to slip through our fingers, mostly on technicalities."

Conroy spoke. "This time we have him on tape making a drug deal with one of our undercover agents.

Of course we always have to worry about his lawyer crying, entrapment." The agent shook his head. "In the past we've had witnesses to his drug activity, but by the time it comes to trial, they've refused to testify for fear of retaliation."

He took a sip of coffee. "We knew Kathryn Archer was living in the compound. We spotted her and the boy walking the grounds, but she was never alone."

Brandon had no idea that Nora had been held against her will.

"When we went in with a warrant she and the boy were gone. And since Alcazar knows where she is, we feel she'd be safer in protective custody."

"I won't be held prisoner again."

They all turned to see Nora come downstairs.

Although the middle of the night, she looked fresh with her hair pulled back into a ponytail, showing off her pretty face and rich blue eyes.

"Mrs. Archer."

"No, I'm Nora Donnelly."

Conroy nodded, then introduced himself and his partner. "Like I was telling Detective Randell, we feel you'd be safer under protection."

She looked at Brandon, unable to hide her hurt. "So you're finally getting rid of me."

"It's for your protection."

She turned back to DEA agents. "Then keep Jimmy in jail. He's a drug dealer for goodness sake!"

"And we need to prove it, with your help. We hear you have a ledger."

"Yes. But before I hand it over I need some guarantees."

"What are they?"

"I'll need protection, especially for my son. He's diabetic so it's imperative he has competent medical personnel watching him."

"He'll have it," Paulson said. "If there was any other way, Ms. Donnelly, I wouldn't put you through this."

"And believe me, if I had a choice, I'd be long gone."

"Then let's go get the ledger."

She shook her head. "I can't leave my son alone."

"I'll stay with him," Brandon volunteered.

Nora met his gaze. "It's not that I don't trust you, but I want him in a safe place."

"We can't arrange for a safe house before tomorrow."

But Brandon knew of a place. "I can keep Nora and Zach at the ranch, in one of the cabins in the valley. It's secluded…there are security cameras and no one gets through the gated area without us knowing about it. You can monitor all activity from our office, see everyone who comes in or goes out." He looked at Nora. "That means nobody is getting to you or Zach. They'll have to go through me first," he finished, hoping he'd sold her on the idea. He wanted to give her peace of mind, and help keep them safe. The ranch was the best plan. He turned to Paulson. "The sheriff's office can assign extra manpower if needed."

"Let me clear this, first," the agent said as he pulled out his cell phone and walked away. "But I don't see a problem. If that's okay with you, Ms. Donnelly?"

"I don't have a choice!"

Nora turned and walked up the steps.

While the agents made their calls, Brandon went after Nora. He followed her to the bedroom, but stopped in the doorway. An ache erupted in his stomach as he eyed the woman whom he'd come to care for so much.

Her gaze rose to meet his eyes. Hell, he was in love with her. And he had a sinking feeling that when the dust cleared, he could lose her.

He swallowed. "You both will be safer if you stay at the ranch. There are a lot of people around to watch out for you. Besides, Zach loves it there."

"I told you before, Brandon, we're not your responsibility."

"This has never been about responsibility, Nora." He closed the space between them and drew her into his arms.

After a moment she moved out of his embrace, blinking at threatening tears. "We both know it can't be about anything else."

CHAPTER TEN

An hour later, along with the two sheriff's deputies as escorts, they drove Brandon and Zach to the cabin. No one was sure if his condo was being watched, so they'd used the darkness as a cover.

Zach hadn't seemed frightened about the change of location, but he definitely was concerned about his mother. The forty-minute drive was pretty quiet, so Brandon was happy to see his dad at the cabin door. The kitchen had already been stocked with food and supplies for however long they needed to stay.

While the deputies checked the place out, one stayed up in the parking area, Brandon set up radio communication and Cade showed Zach the movie video selection.

By noon everything was in place for their stay, and the seven-year-old had been fed. Now he sat in front of a small television watching cartoons. Brandon checked his blood sugar and was happy to see it was in the normal range.

He sat down in the chair and watched the sullen child. "Are you feeling all right?"

"Yeah." Zach turned to him. "Is my mom really coming back?"

"Yes, of course she is."

He seemed to mull it over, then asked, "Can we go see Hawk's Flame."

"Not today, partner. We need to stay close to the cabin." He wasn't even sure he should take the boy outside at all, so he expected cabin fever to set in eventually.

Zach studied him. "There isn't going to be another time, 'cause I have to go back to my dad."

"No, Zach, you're not going back. You're never going to have to live with him again," Brandon assured him. "But I can't lie to you—there's a chance you might have to go back to San Diego so your mother can talk to the police."

"Is she in trouble 'cause she took the money?"

"No, son." He sat down on the floor. "She's trying to help the police."

"So my dad can't get out of jail. Ever?" the boy said, frowning. "He's mean to me and mom. He hit her and one time he locked me in my room. Mom got scared 'cause I didn't have my medicine."

Brandon tried to stay calm, but it was difficult. How was he supposed to let them leave, knowing they could possibly be in danger? "Your father will never hurt you or your mom ever again. But you need to tell the judge everything that happened."

"I'm scared."

"I know it's hard, Zach. It was for me, too. When I

was your age, I had to tell the police that my stepfather was mean to my mother."

"But Cade is your dad."

How could he explain this? "He's my real father but he didn't come to know about me until I was about your age, when he married my mom. And even though I did things that weren't always good, Cade never raised a hand to me. He's the best dad ever. And that's what you deserve, too, Zach."

The boy looked hopeful as he glanced up at Brandon. "I wish you could be my dad. So I can stay here forever."

Brandon's gut tightened as he spoke of his own feelings. "I want that, too, Zach. But other things have to happen first."

"Grown-up stuff, huh?"

He smiled. "Yeah, but I'm working on it, partner. I'm workin' on it." No way was he giving up on the boy, or his mother.

The boy's big brown eyes stared up at him. "You promise?"

"I promise."

The door opened and Nora walked in. Zach jumped to his feet and ran into her open arms. "Mom, you're here."

She smiled. "Yes, I am."

"I wasn't scared 'cause Brandon said he'd take care of us."

"Well, that's nice of him."

Nora glanced across the room at Brandon. He looked as tired as she felt. After she'd left this morning, she'd retrieved the ledger from the locker, and gladly gave it over to the agents. They'd taken her to the sheriff's office where she was surprised to find a lawyer waiting for her. A Clinton Maxwell, who was a friend of the Randell family.

Nora insisted she couldn't afford him, but Mr. Maxwell only smiled and said he was working pro bono. Once they sat down and she'd been peppered with questions, she was glad for the lawyer's presence.

Brandon walked to her. "Zach, why don't you go back to your cartoons so I can talk to your mother."

When the boy ran off, Nora wanted to call him back, but knew she had to face Brandon. No matter how hard this time together was, it was all she had left. And she was going to cherish every last bit of time with Brandon here, while knowing it would hurt to say goodbye.

Early the next morning, Nora walked out of the cabin carrying her coffee mug. Since Zach had eaten and was watching a video, and Brandon was in the shower, she'd decided to steal a moment for herself. She had to get out of the close confines even for a little while.

Bundled in one of Brandon's University of Texas sweatshirts and Abby's borrowed jeans, she wandered through the dew-covered grass. Following the rhythmic sound of the creek and chirping birds, she made her way down the rise to the meadow below.

Once through the trees she was met by the bright

October sun. That was where she spotted the first of the ponies; the buckskin mare with her foal.

Nora stood still as the animal raised its head and looked at her. They both froze. Nora's heart pounded, afraid she'd frighten them off. After all, she was the one intruding in their space. Finally dismissing her as a threat, the mare went back to grazing.

Nora leaned against a trunk and took a sip of her coffee, wishing she could feel as peaceful. Coming to the cabin yesterday and spending the evening with Brandon and Zach had made her forget for a short time. Despite Brandon's assurance that he was going to keep her safe, she hadn't been able to push aside the severity of her problems, or her total mess of a life. She had no job, and no place to live, but that was the easy part.

The worst was, a notorious drug dealer was after her. Jimmy wanted what she had, or what she used to have. Hopefully the ledger would be enough evidence to put the man away for life.

Nora glanced back up the hill and spotted the man standing in the parking lot, another deputy assigned to watch over her and Zach, to keep them safe until the DEA agents decided where they wanted her. Then what? The witness protection program?

She turned back to the mustangs. She didn't care about herself, but what kind of life was this for her child? Zach deserved more. Tears filled her eyes; her lips trembled as she wiped her sleeve across her cheeks. And there would be no more Brandon in her life.

She thought back to their few nights together. Not

together, like she wanted. She wanted to know what it was like to lay in his arms, and allowed herself to feel what it was like to have a man love her. To touch her, caress her with a loving hand, giving her pleasure that she'd never known existed. Another tear fell. It only made it harder for her to leave, and even harder to forget him.

She heard her name and quickly wiped the moisture from her face and put on a smile before she turned around.

Brandon was wearing a pair of worn jeans, a long-sleeved, gray Henley T-shirt, but no familiar, sexy grin. A funny feeling erupted in her stomach as he came down the hill toward her. He didn't look happy.

"You aren't supposed to be out here." He glanced around and waved at the man up on the ridge. "It's dangerous."

"My whole life is dangerous." It had been hard to sit across a breakfast table from the man, pretending everything was normal. "Sorry, the view stole me away. I could get used to this."

Brandon could see the evidence of Nora's tears. He couldn't blame her for having an overflow of emotions. It had been a rough few months for her and Zach. It had been a rough life period. He only wished he could give her more.

"I'm glad you like it so much. It's yours and Zach's anytime you want to come here."

She shook her head vigorously. "No, when we leave here we won't be back."

His chest tightened. "Why, Nora? Why can't you come back?"

She tossed the last of her coffee in the grass. "Because when I go back to testify it could take a long time. And it might not be safe for us to return here."

Brandon had been trying to figure out a way to make things easier for her. "About that, I've been talking with the agents. There's a slim chance you might not have to testify. Technically the ledger was in the wall safe, so it was missing evidence." He shrugged. "And you've been cooperating."

She sighed. "As much as I want to believe that everything is going to work out, I still have Jimmy out there wanting revenge. He'll know I gave the ledger to the DEA. And he'll want me punished."

"I'm not going to let him get to you or Zach, Nora. I care so much for you both." He pushed it further. "And you can't deny you have feelings for me."

She tried to look away, but he refused to let her hide.

"It's true, Nora. But you have to believe that we can get through this. Together."

Her gaze met his as she lifted her hand to his face. "Oh, Brandon, you'll never know how much that means to me, but you can't get any more involved in this problem. Please."

She closed her eyes momentarily.

Brandon wanted to argue, but he couldn't cause her any more stress. "Okay, we have such little time left so why can't we just pretend that we're at the most perfect place ever in the world?" He touched her cheek. "And nothing can touch us."

"Oh, Brandon," she sighed.

He put on a smile. "It's just you and me, Nora. In this special place," he breathed as he dipped his head toward her and brushed his lips over her surprised mouth. Once, twice, and the third time the kiss suddenly turned intense and hungry. He also hoped it would prove how much he needed her in his life.

She finally pushed him away, trying to catch her breath. "No, I can't change my mind." She looked troubled. "When they come for me I still have to leave. And I have to get through this before I can think of anything else."

When he stepped forward, she raised her hand. "Don't make this any harder. There can't be any you and me, and wishing isn't going to make it happen."

He knew she was lying. She wanted a future with him, too. "So we go back to business for now?"

"I agreed to stay here in the first place because of Zach. He has always been my first concern."

It still hurt. "Zach is my concern, too. So are you."

"So then understand that I can't handle any more pressure now. I need to think only about surviving this. I can't think about you, or what could have been. I'm sorry. I'm so sorry."

She swung around and hurried up the hill, and soon right out of Brandon's life.

Later that day, Hank stopped by the cabin. He could see Nora's misery as soon as he walked in the door.

"You sure aren't good advertising for our get-away cabins," he said. "They were built to help people relax."

She looked at him from the small table in front of the picture window. Her sadness touched his heart.

"I'm sorry," she said, trying to brighten.

Hank walked across the large room's open concept with high-beamed ceilings. There was a huge fireplace and a seating area with overstuffed furniture, and plush rugs to lie down on and snuggle up with a loved one. The isolated cabins had been rented many times as honeymoon suites. He only hoped his grandson and Nora would get a chance to use it as that someday. But they had a lot of hurdles to get over first.

Hank sat down across from Nora, who was pretending to watch her son with Brandon just outside on the porch.

"How are you holding up?"

She put a smile on her pretty face. "I'm fine," she told him. "I'm sorry, Hank, that I involved your family in my mess."

He smiled. "Land sake's, darlin', you should get Brandon to tell you a bit about our family history. Over the generations, the Randell men have stood on both sides of the law. And my boys have gotten into plenty of messes." He shook his head. "They're not proud of it, but we've all managed to survive."

"This is different, Hank. This is dangerous."

He shook his head. "Neither you nor that boy of yours had anything to do with your ex-husband's illegal business. Unless you're playing the victim." He studied her. "And you don't look like the type. Not someone who risked everything to take her son to safety." He leaned forward and rested his arms on the table. "I've spent time with your Zach. What a fine young man you're raising. You have to be so proud."

She nodded, biting her lip to hold back her emotions. "I am. He's had to go through so much."

"And it's made him stronger, but he gets that from you, Nora." He patted her hand. "But it's all right to ask for help, too. Just so you know, we're here for you both. So is Brandon."

"Oh, Hank, I know what kind of man Brandon is. That's what makes it so hard to leave him."

"So don't give up on your man, because he hasn't given up on you."

Back in the cabin, Brandon had spent much of the day and evening on the phone with his boss, the sheriff and with Benjamin Mathis, the federal prosecutor in San Diego. The DEA had gone over the ledger, trying to build a case against Jimmy Archer. It wasn't going to be easy. Jimmy's ledger had more incriminating details on his associates than himself. The authorities had issued arrest warrants for several drug dealers in the area. At least the ledger was helping fight crime.

Brandon held out the phone to Nora. "Mathis wants to speak to you."

Nora took the phone. "Yes, Mr. Mathis." She wanted to get this over with. She had to get away from Brandon.

"Ms. Donnelly. We're going to need you to return to San Diego as soon as possible. We've arranged for a safe house for you and your son. There are details we need to go through before we take our case to a judge."

"Of course, Mr. Mathis." This had been what she wanted, but now that it was going to happen it was frightening. "When do you need me?"

Brandon swung around and shot her an intense look. She had to turn away. "I'm sorry, what was that again?"

"I said, tomorrow?"

"If you can arrange safe travel for me and my son, tomorrow would be fine." He gave her more details about the agent and her escort. She wrote them down, but her mind wasn't on anything but the man across the room. The man she loved, but could never build a life with.

Finally she handed the cell phone back to Brandon. "Looks like I'll be out of your hair by tomorrow."

He blew out a breath. "It's not as if it wasn't expected, but just not this soon."

The wood in the fireplace crackled and sparks danced in the dim room. With her son tucked in bed in the other room, it was just the two of them. And she wanted nothing more than to go into Brandon's arms, and let him kiss away her fears and loneliness.

"It's better this way, Brandon."

"We both know that's a lie, Nora. The difference is you won't let me in to help."

She couldn't deny that, but her aching body betrayed her. "Let me get through this, Brandon. It's hard enough, without worrying about you, too."

"And you don't think I won't worry about you?"

"I don't have to anymore. Maybe you should forget I ever came here. It might be the only choice if we want to stay safe."

Nora watched his jaw tighten. "Sure, it'll be easy. I'll just forget those sparkling blue eyes, a mouth that causes me to ache. That should be easy." He threw up his hands in frustration and started for the door.

Nora felt her panic building. She couldn't let him go—not like this.

"Brandon!" she called.

He stopped and turned around and all she could do was run into his arms.

Without saying another word, his head lowered and his mouth captured hers. Hunger, desire and need all surfaced as he carried her to the fireplace and laid her down on the plush rug.

Never had there been anyone who made her feel this kind of longing. This kind of need. She reached out and her fingertips came in contact with his chest.

A shiver went through her as she ran her palms over his solid strength. She worked frantically at tugging his shirt until the barrier finally disappeared and she made contact with his heated skin. Her sweatshirt disappeared, too, and she moved closer and pressed her body to his.

"Nora."

She heard her name spoken on a hoarse whisper and slowly she opened her eyes and looked into Brandon's face. He was lying beside her on the soft rug, his gaze intense, smoldering. He cupped her face with his palms. "I want you to be sure you know what you're doing."

Nora's heart was pounding in her chest, an ache in her lower stomach that only this man could satisfy. She should stop, but she couldn't. Just once, she wanted to close everything out, except for the two of them.

"I want you, Brandon Randell."

"I want to make love to you, too, Nora." He lowered his head and took her mouth in another hungry kiss. He released her and trailed kisses along her jaw to her ear, sending more chills down her spine.

"Oh, Brandon," she gasped.

He looked at her. "I want to make this night perfect for you. Tell me what you want."

"Only you, Brandon," she managed to whisper, and silently added, forever.

She pulled his head down to hers and pressed a kiss against his mouth. "Just for the time we have left. Make me forget."

She closed her eyes and emptied her head of everything but this man. He had saved her more times than she could count. She wanted one last, special moment with him.

Then she had to save herself.

CHAPTER ELEVEN

JUST before dawn the following morning, Brandon found himself alone in front of the dying fire. He sat up and glanced around the silent cabin.

Nora. No, she wouldn't leave like this. He pushed aside the blankets, stood and pulled on his jeans and shirt from off the floor. While working the zipper, he checked the bedroom to find Zach still asleep, but no Nora. In the kitchen, the light over the stove showed the area was deserted, too.

Panic surged through him as he rushed to the front door and pulled it open. He stopped quickly when he found her perched against the porch railing. Wrapped in a blanket, she stared out at the valley.

He released a long breath, enjoying the sight of her. Her beautiful, thick hair hung past her shoulders. His sweatshirt covered a lot of her, but left those gorgeous legs exposed, triggering memories of last night. Just a few hours ago, she'd been in his arms. They'd shared an intimacy he'd never known before, and couldn't imagine sharing with anyone but her. Yet even after their passionate night, he knew she had to leave him.

What frightened him the most was it might be for good.

And he couldn't stop her. His chest tightened with an ache that made it difficult to breath.

Nora looked over her shoulder. "Sorry, I was lost in this incredible view." She sighed. "You're so lucky to have this place."

He wanted to tell her she could come here anytime. She could live right here. If only she would stay. "I know. Did I tell you before my parents got together, I ran away and came here? The idea was to get Mom and Dad to come find me."

She glanced over her shoulder and gave him a faint smile. "Why am I not surprised?"

"It wasn't for attention. I only wanted my parents to stop fighting and get married so Cade would be my dad." He recalled that long ago time. "What I didn't expect was for it to rain like a son of a gun, and I got cold and wet. Plus the punishment I got for leaving by myself."

"How old were you?"

"About Zach's age. But all I could think about was wanting a dad." He came up behind her. "Family is important to me, Nora. I want to give that to you and Zach. I want you both, Nora."

She pushed off the railing and moved away from him. "You want promises, Brandon, and I can't give you any."

"I just want to be included in a future with you, wherever that might be. Right here would be nice."

"I'm not sure I would fit in here."

"Come on, Nora. You already do."

She smiled softly. "Your family has been gracious to me and Zach, but there are issues with my past. We've had very different childhoods. I've never had a family like you do. No father, and after my grandmother passed away, it was just me and my mom for a long time. Then when I was fourteen she died in a car accident, and I became a ward of the state."

"I'm sorry," he told her.

She nodded and looked toward the ponies wandering in toward the creek. "That's where I first met Jimmy. We were both in the same group home. He was a few years older and offered to show me the ropes. We got into a few scrapes together, some shoplifting, and vandalism. Nothing serious. I got over my attitude and anger and the police said my record was sealed. Then one day I got home from school and Jimmy was gone. No one said what happened, but I figured he'd gotten into more trouble."

He knew about her juvenile record, but he was still surprised by her confession. Brandon came around the railing to face her. "Why are you telling me this now?"

"I ran into Jimmy years later after I graduated from nursing school. He seemed different from when we were kids. He was polished and had become a successful businessman." She glanced down at the ground. "Maybe I deserved what happened to me."

"That's not true and you know it. You would never have gotten involved with him if you knew what he was into."

"How do you know that?" she argued.

"Because I've come to know you, Nora. I've seen what kind of nurse you are, and what kind of mother you are. You've worked too hard to make a better life for Zach and to get away from Jimmy."

"I've made a mess of everything. I still might never have that life."

He reached out and drew her into his arms. "I'm going to make sure you get that life, Nora. You, me and Zach."

He felt her trembling as she clutched his shirt. "Oh, Brandon. Please, don't do this…don't make this any harder—"

He cut off her words as his mouth covered hers. It didn't take long for their hunger to ignite sparks between them, creating a need that had him forgetting everything else but this woman.

Nora suddenly pulled away. "Stop. Please." She shut her eyes, fighting tears. "I need to concentrate on surviving this. There's no room for anything else. I can't let my hopes get raised."

He hated seeing her pain. "All I want is to help you."

"Then let me go, Brandon. It's the only way."

It had been more than a week since Nora left the ranch with federal agents. All Brandon had were the memories of their time together. The days and the nights he'd spent with her. Now, every minute away from her was eating at him.

When the time came, Nora had given him a quick goodbye, unable to look him in the eye, but Zach had hung back and hugged Brandon, clutching him like a lifeline.

"I love you, Brandon," he whispered.

"I love you, too, son. If ever you need me, just call." He pressed his business card into the small hand. "I'll be there."

Zach nodded.

Then Nora called her son's name.

"I got to go. Bye." The boy ran out the door.

Brandon fought going after them both, but managed to stay put.

Every day he went to work as if nothing had happened, as if his world hadn't crashed down around him. He tried, but nothing could distract him enough to forget her. He tried to get information about her case, but couldn't. It was too high profile, and too much was at stake to leak anything. That worried him, too, wondering if Nora had already gone into witness protection.

By the end of the week, Brandon had annoyed everyone in the office, so his captain told him to take time off and sent him home.

Being idle was worse. He had too much time to think about Nora and Zach's safety. He should have ignored her wishes and escorted her back to San Diego. Maybe he could have worked out a deal with the D.A. to act as her bodyguard, but she would have hated him for that. Now, she was hundreds of miles away.

Brandon walked out into the corral at the ranch, trying to stay busy and not think. Nothing helped.

"Hey, I thought you came out here to work," his dad called from the barn door. Alongside him were his uncles, Travis and Chance. They intended to mend fences this morning and had roped him into going along.

"I'm ready whenever you are."

"Seems to me," Travis began, "he's going to be worthless if his mind can't stay on his work."

Brandon knew his uncles were going to give him a bad time. It was their way to distract him. "Since when do you need to think to string fencing?"

The three brothers caught up with him. "Ask your dad," Chance said, sending Cade a knowing look. "Seems he had a little disagreement with your mother and ended up wrapping himself in barbed wire."

His uncle's jibe got him a punch in the arm from Cade. "There's no reason to give out details."

Chance held up his arms. "I'm just sayin', women can mess with your mind, and one distraction can be hazardous. We've all been there."

"My son already knows that," Cade began. "You two were supposed to come by today to help cheer him up."

Travis stepped in. "The only thing that's going to cheer up Brandon is going after Nora."

"And that's out of the question," Cade admitted.

The three Randell men turned to each other, ignoring Brandon altogether.

"Who says he can't?" Travis asked. "There's no law he can't go to San Diego. The last I looked this was still a free country. In fact, we all could go." A grin appeared as he snapped his fingers. "Hey, I bet we could even get cousin Brady to fly us there. He's probably itchin' to go somewhere outside the local airports to bring in the tourists."

Brandon could only watch his uncles. He knew so many stories of how close they'd been growing up, fighting controversy about their cattle-rustling father. Over the years they'd had brushes with the law, and their neighbors, until Hank took them in and raised them. They'd ended up stronger, successful and still together. And he was so lucky to have them.

They finally turned to him and his dad spoke. "A lot of years ago, son, I gave up on your mother, and I was wrong not to fight for her. I'll never forgive myself for the eight years we lost. I was lucky to get a second chance with you both."

Travis stepped in. "Yeah, we've all needed second chances."

Cade glared at his younger brother's comment, then turned back to his son. "I know this situation with Nora seems different, but not so much. Women say they don't need you when they really do. It's not so much a big, strong guy coming to save the day, but more like they want to know you're with them. That you have their back. So if you love Nora, then you need to go be with her."

"Nora doesn't want me there."

Cade glanced at his brothers, then back at his son. "Look, son, there were so many times I left your mother alone because she asked me to. Later, I learned she really wanted me to come after her." His dad pushed his hat back off his forehead. "I know it would be so much easier if they'd just say what they mean. But they don't always."

"Because we want you to figure it out for yourselves."

Turning, they saw Abby Randell had arrived in the corral, along with Hank.

Cade went to his wife. "Now, honey, you know I've tried and I still mess up."

She reached up and kissed him. "And I appreciate the effort."

Brandon saw the secret look they exchanged, leaving no doubt how much they loved each other. He wanted that with Nora.

His mother turned to him. "We know you're hurting right now, son. But you have to think about Nora. She has a lot to get through, but I have confidence that she will. I also believe that if it's possible, she will find her way back to you."

Brandon looked at his grandfather for help. "What if Nora can't come back? What if she and Zach have to go into witness protection?"

The patriarch of the family looked every bit his age today. "Son, I wish I had the answer you want to hear, but I don't. All I know is love is a mighty strong emotion. You're a Randell, and from what I've seen over the years, Randell men love for a lifetime. So I have faith that if Nora can't find a way back to you, you'll find a way to her." He glanced around at his own sons. "That's always been the way of this family."

Two days later, on a cold, overcast morning, Nora sat in the prosecutor's office while Zach was under close watch in a safe location away from the courthouse.

Was it enough security for her son?

She stood and started to pace. Since her return, there hadn't been any trouble. She gone over and over her testimony, and now she just wanted it over with. Although Jimmy knew she was back to testify, he hadn't made any trouble for her about taking Zach out of state. As far as the feds were concerned, they were just happy to have the ledger and her help in convicting Jimmy.

She was willing to cooperate with the court; not that she had much to tell, but she had to keep Jimmy in jail. This would be her only chance, and she had to take the risk.

Nora's thoughts turned to Brandon. She had to give him up. Witness protection seemed to be the only chance she had to survive Jimmy's threats, and keep him out of their lives.

That meant she would have to keep Brandon out, too.

Nora sighed. It had been so hard to leave him. To have to pretend that he hadn't mattered to her, that she hadn't wanted everything he offered her, especially his love. She brushed away a tear, feeling the dull ache in her chest. She couldn't drag Brandon into her mess. It had to end.

Suddenly the office door opened and Mr. Mathis rushed in. She released a long breath. Okay, she could do this. "Is it time to go?"

The prosecutor shook his head, then a half smile appeared. "Seems we don't need your testimony after all, Ms. Donnelly."

Panic hit her hard. "Why? Please don't tell me Jimmy's lawyer got him off."

He shook his head. "Not this time. I believe this time one of his business associates took care of the problem. Jimmy Archer was stabbed and killed by another inmate."

The sound of the phone ringing jerked Brandon from sleep. He rolled over in bed and reached for the receiver, reading the clock: 1:15 a.m.

With a groan, he answered, "Randell."

"Brandon," Nora said in a quiet voice.

He sat up, shaking the sleep from his head and praying he wasn't dreaming. "Nora? Are you all right?"

"I'm fine."

After hearing the news yesterday about Archer's death, he'd tried to call her. But even his law enforcement connections hadn't gotten him anywhere. The federal prosecutor wouldn't give out Nora's location, or a way to get hold of her.

"Are you sure?"

"Yes, both Zach and I are doing well, considering."

It had been three weeks since she and Zach left San Angelo to testify, and it had taken everything in him not to go after her. Now it was finally over.

He climbed out of bed. "Look, Nora, I can be on a plane in a matter of hours. Just tell me where to meet you."

"That's why I'm calling you, Brandon. I don't want you to come here."

He froze, then raked his fingers through his hair. "You don't mean that, Nora. I don't want you to go through this alone."

There was a long pause, and then she spoke. "I have

to, Brandon. With all the legal mess here, I need time to sort through it."

"Okay, I understand that. Red tape can be a bear," he said, but he felt there was more.

"I need more, Brandon. I need time. Time for me to heal, time for Zach, knowing that whatever I decide, my son will need to come first. And before I can think of a future, I have to face my past."

Brandon's heart constricted. He was losing her. "I'll let you do that, Nora. I just want to be there for you."

"I know you do," she stressed with tears in her voice. "But I need to do it by myself. For so long Jimmy's controlled everything. Some things I need to do on my own. This is one of them. I want to be whole before I come back to you."

"You're perfect to me."

"But not to me." She sighed. "Just so you know, leaving you that morning was one of the hardest things I've ever done. The second hardest is making this call. Please, Brandon, try to understand I need to find me right now."

He didn't want to understand, but he didn't have a choice. "So are you ever coming back?"

"I want to. More than you can imagine," she told him. "That's what I'm working on, Brandon. I've got to go."

Before he could ask for her number, the phone went dead silent. He closed his eyes, wishing he could have said the magic words to bring her back.

Angrily he paced the room. He wanted to throw something, to slam his fist through a wall. To say the heck with it. He didn't need her in his life.

First of all, he had to stop loving Nora Donnelly, and that wasn't about to happen anytime soon.

Many times over the next two weeks, Brandon had run Nora's words through his head, and his anger turned to hurt until he realized how pathetic he'd become. If she didn't want to come back to him, he would have to live with that. It was time he got on with his own life.

To start, he had his job with the sheriff's office. He'd stay busy with investigations. The regular trips out to the ranch on his days off took care of filling the empty times. Hard physical work had distracted him, at least during the days. He hadn't figured out the nights, yet. His family had been there, too, helping him through this. That included his mother, calling him today and inviting him to lunch. It was her excuse to check up on him.

He climbed out of his truck and headed up the walkway to the door of the women's shelter. As he passed the garden, he couldn't help but think about the time he'd been here with Nora. Did everything have to remind him of her?

With a sigh, he pressed the intercom button and waited as the receptionist buzzed him inside. He put on a smile as he walked toward Bess. "How's my favorite gal?" he teased.

She cocked an eyebrow. "I'm on to your sweet-talking, Detective Randell. I know you just want my oatmeal cookies."

"You got me," he said. "Does that mean I'm still on your list?"

She came around her desk. "I'd be foolish to turn away a handsome devil like you." She winked. "Stop by on your way out and I'll have a bag with your name on it. Although, I doubt your mind will be on cookies."

Brandon frowned. He had no idea what she meant by that. "Bess, have you seen my mother?"

She smiled. "I'm to send you to the garden room."

"Thanks," he called as he took off down the hall. The sooner he had lunch, the sooner he'd be back at work. Although it was his day off, there were a number of unsolved cases on his desk. He planned to put in overtime this weekend to catch up.

He knocked on the door, then stepped in. Inside, the room was empty. Then his attention went to the French doors where there was an auburn-haired woman standing on the patio. Her back was to him, but there was something familiar about her. When she turned around, his heart stopped.

Nora. Immediately his pulse shot up as his gaze combed over her. She was thinner, but she still had plenty of curves to fill out her navy trousers and blue pullover sweater. She gave him a hesitant smile and stepped through the double doors into the room.

"Brandon."

His gaze locked with those sapphire eyes that had mesmerized him from their first meeting. They were working overtime now. He ached to go to her, but he held back. "So you're back."

For a second, Nora felt nervous, and questioned returning to San Angelo. Seeing Brandon again was hard. How she wished he'd just open his arms to her. But she couldn't expect that.

Then another second passed and she finally spoke.

"I returned yesterday."

He stiffened more. "I guess I'm not at the top of your list."

She deserved that, but it still hurt. "You know I had to stay in San Diego for a while. Zach is Jimmy's heir, and everything was left to him. Not all the money he made was illegal."

"Please, don't try to tell me the man had an ounce of decency."

"No, but my son deserves what is his. For his future."

"Seems to me, I offered you both a future, but you decided that it wasn't what you wanted. Then suddenly you're back and what am I supposed to do? Listen to you tell me about your ex?" He shook his head. "I can't do it, Nora. So if you came here to say you've decided to stay in San Diego, you could have put that in an e-mail." He turned to leave.

"I always wanted you, Brandon," she called as he reached the door. "And you know I had to stay there, but as you can see I'm here now."

He turned around and waited for her to say more.

"I came to the shelter for a reason. I was abused by Jimmy. For a long time, I was ashamed of that, that I let him control me. Both Zach and I have been in counseling for the past few weeks. I'm trying to put my life back together. I know if I came back to you, I needed to be whole again." She fought tears. "I want to be the woman you deserve."

He came toward her. "Why don't you let me be the judge of that?"

"No, Brandon, I had to be strong on my own. Whether you know it or not, you Randell men have a tendency to want to take over and fix everything. I needed to fix me, myself."

"You didn't need fixing."

"Thank you. But I still had to deal with my past."

A touch of a smile twitched at the corners of his mouth. "You are different, and it's not just your hair. I take it you were coloring it so you wouldn't be recognized."

"Didn't do much good." She brushed the strands off her shoulder. "Do you hate redheads?"

"You're kidding, right? There's nothing about you I could hate."

She bit down on her lower lip to keep from falling apart. "I'm glad. I inherited it from my Irish grandmother."

Brandon's gaze locked with hers. "So where do we go from here?"

This was the hard part. "I hope we can move forward."

He sighed, his voice lowered. "That depends on you, Nora. You already know how I feel."

"That's what kept me going every single day." She hated the trembling in her voice, the dryness in her throat. He just stood there looking gorgeous with those dark bedroom eyes and sexy smile. "Do all you Randells have to be so darn sure of yourselves?"

He came closer. "You have no idea how unsteady I feel right now," he murmured. "Now getting back to why you returned…"

She swallowed hard. "Because of you, Brandon Randell. I love you and want to build a life with you."

He tossed his hat on the desk and gripped her arms.

His mouth closed over hers so swiftly she could only gasp. When he deepened the kiss, their passion took over as his arms went around her, pulling her against him.

Brandon groaned when he broke off the kiss. "God, Nora. I was so afraid I'd lost you."

"I'm sorry, Brandon." Her hand touched his jaw. "I had to do some healing first, before I could tell you how I feel."

"I love you, Nora Donnelly." He kissed her over and over. "Just don't leave me again. I need you in my life."

Suddenly Brandon realized only one thing could make this day more perfect. He dropped to one knee, and watched her eyes widen in surprise. "I know we've only known each other a short while," he began, trying to hide his nervousness. "But I knew from the first time I saw you that you were everything I've ever wanted in a partner, a lover, a wife. I never thought I'd feel like this about anyone. Will you marry me, Nora?"

She nodded and pulled him up, then went into his arms. "Oh, yes, Brandon, I'll marry you."

With a loud whoop, he swung her around in a circle. By the time he sat her down they were both dizzy. "And Zach," he said. "I want to be his dad, Nora. I want him to be able to depend on me to be there for him, to teach him to ride a horse, to love the land." He raised a hand to stop any protest. "I know there could be problems with his diabetes, but we can handle it together. Most importantly, I want Zach to have the chance to be a normal kid. I couldn't love him any more if he were mine." He swallowed hard. "Do you think I could adopt him?"

Nora trembled as her fingers touched her mouth. "Maybe you should ask him." She nodded toward the door to where her son stood with Abby and Cade Randell.

Brandon nodded at his parents who couldn't hide their happiness. He then went to the little boy, who looked excited and bewildered at the same time.

"Hey, partner, hi," Brandon said as crouched down in front of him.

Zach nodded. "You want to 'dopt me?"

Brandon felt a well of emotions and nodded.

"You'd really be my dad?"

"Yeah, but only if that's what you want, too. You can think about it for—"

The boy launched himself into Brandon's arms and he had to catch himself to keep from falling backward. "No, I want you to be my dad."

"And I want you to be my son." Brandon glanced up at his own father and mother. There were tears in their eyes. He knew they were remembering years ago when Brandon learned that Cade was his biological dad.

Zach pulled back, and Brandon brushed at the tears on the boy's cheeks. "So, you like the idea of me marrying your mom?"

"Yeah, 'cause she was really sad since we had to go away."

He looked back at Nora. "I'll see what I can do to make her happy again."

"She likes it when you kiss her," Zach volunteered.

Brandon grinned and went to his future wife. "That makes me happy, too."

His mom and dad joined the group. "Hey, Zach, maybe we should go and leave the happy couple to make plans." His mother hugged Brandon. "Congratulations, son. We're so happy for you. Not only do we get a daughter-in-law, but our first grandson." She then hugged Nora, whispered something to her and both women laughed.

His dad slapped him on his back. "I guess your mother was right. Nora needed to come back to you." He shook his head as they watched the two lovely women together. "Another redhead." Cade fought a grin. "Things will never get dull, that's for sure."

Brandon had to agree.

Abby released Nora and took hold of Zach's hand. "We're headed for the cafeteria, maybe you two will want to join us for lunch, later." She shrugged. "Or maybe not. Come on, Grandson. It's Grandpa's treat."

The threesome walked out, leaving the couple alone. Brandon drew Nora in his arms. "Looks like we need to make some plans. And I'm thinking it could take a while, maybe all night." He grinned. "Do you think Grandma and Grandpa will babysit tonight?"

"I think your parents will do anything to help the wedding along, since your mom's the one who helped get me back here."

Brandon was glad his mother and Nora were becoming close. After all, they were the two most important women in his life. "I'm glad she could be there for you. By the way what did she say to you that made you laugh? Some deep dark secret about me?"

Nora slid her hands up Brandon's chest and around his neck. "Just what I already knew—that Randell men are hard to resist."

"Good, then I have an advantage here." He hugged her close. "Does that mean I can have my way with you?"

"As long as I can have my way with you."

He kissed her until they weren't thinking much at all except how wonderful it was that they'd found their way back together. "For a lifetime, Nora. And that's not nearly enough time."

EPILOGUE

NORA stepped outside to the cabin porch. She drew in a relaxing breath, enjoying the fresh, earthy smell. There was nothing like springtime in Mustang Valley.

Well, maybe a few things. She glanced at the platinum rings on her finger—a diamond engagement ring along with the matching wedding band. It had been seven months since she returned to Texas, and two months since she'd become Mrs. Brandon Randell in a small church ceremony just a few miles from the valley. Cade and Abby hosted the reception back at the ranch with family and friends.

The honeymoon had been the only thing they'd had to compromise on. They'd taken a long weekend, wanting to stay close to home. Millie had offered to stay with Zach, and Brandon and Nora agreed that as long as they were together it would be a perfect honeymoon.

During their wedding night at the secluded cabin she'd stayed in before, Brandon had shown her how much he loved and cherished her. They'd also shared much of their past as well as plans for their future together, and both definitely wanted more children.

Nora hadn't returned to work at the hospital. Instead she chose to volunteer at Hidden Haven House. She wanted to help other abused women find their way to freedom and independence. It helped her, too. She'd joined a group session to continue her own therapy. For the first time in years, she was stronger, and happier. Her past was where it was supposed to be: behind her.

A breeze brushed against Nora's cheek as she heard voices. She looked toward the ridge and smiled as she caught sight of the riders. Brandon, atop Shadow, and Zach, not far behind on the mare, Suzy Q.

A lump lodged in her throat at the sight of her son happy and confident on his horse. Amazingly, in the past months, he'd grown an inch and put on much needed weight. Most importantly, his diabetes was under control.

"Hey, Mom," he called as he rode up to the porch. "Grandpa Hank said I could help with the mustang roundup this year. But I have to okay it with you and Dad." He gave her his best grin. "Please, Mom, can I?"

The normal panic set in; she immediately wanted to protect her child. She turned to Brandon. He was dressed in his familiar worn jeans, a Henley shirt that hugged those broad shoulders and a cowboy hat cocked just right. He wasn't only a good-looking man with a sexy grin, but he also played an active role as Zach's father.

It was such a relief that she didn't have to deal with these decisions alone. "What does your father say?"

"I said we'd discuss it." Brandon swung his leg over

the horse and jumped to the ground. He gave her that secret look. "Discussion" was a word that usually got them some private time alone in their bedroom.

"Sounds like a plan," she smiled.

"Ah gee, Mom," Zach complained as he dismounted his horse. "You have to let me go. I'm eight years old now. The other kids will make fun of me."

Brandon could only grin. A year ago, he'd never dreamed this would be his life. He had a wife and child. He'd even moved them all back to the ranch house to start their life together as a family. It hadn't taken long to realize that was where he was meant to be. He still worked as a detective for the sheriff's office, but he'd also decided to go back to school for his law degree. He wanted to help abused women. Women needed a voice, and more rights to protect them from men like Jimmy Archer.

He couldn't have prevented what had happened to his mother or Nora, but maybe he could help other women.

Maybe someday, he might even run for public office.

He looked at his wife. Nora was stronger now, but he also knew there were still bad times when memories crept in. He made sure he was there for her, like his dad had been there for his mother. That was what being a family meant. He still couldn't believe Nora and Zach were his family now and he would always look after them.

He turned to his son. "Zach, you better go inside and get your duffel bag. Uncle Chance will be here soon." They'd planned to work with Hawk's Flame, and the colt was stabled at Chance's place for now.

"What about Suzy Q?"

"I'll get her back to the barn." He smiled at Nora. "Maybe your mother will ride her."

Nora's head shot up. She wasn't exactly fond of horseback riding, yet. "I thought we were going to spend the weekend here?" She gave him one of those seductive smiles.

He hadn't forgotten his weekend alone with his beautiful wife. "I guess it wouldn't hurt to let them spend the night in the lean-to. The weather is warm enough and there's plenty of feed."

"You want me to help?" Zach asked.

He was still a mite too young and inexperienced to handle a horse on his own.

"That's okay, son. I can do it."

Zach handed his reins to Brandon, and headed inside when his mother called to him. "Don't forget to test your blood sugar." The boy had started wearing a pump that did a much easier job of regulating the insulin.

The boy turned around. "I know, Mom. I'm not a baby."

Brandon didn't like the boy's attitude. "Zach, your mother is only concerned about you, and no matter how old you get, she's going to worry."

"You mean like Grandma Abby does with you?"

"Yep, just like my mother does. Believe me it's nice to have that."

Zach nodded. "I'm sorry, Mom." He walked back to her and gave her a hug. "I'll be careful and while I'm at Aunt Joy and Uncle Chance's I'll make sure I check it, too."

She held on tight to her son. "I know you will. I

keep forgetting how grown up you are. You've had to handle so much…"

"Don't, Mom," the eight-year-old chided. "Don't think about before in San Diego. We've got Brandon now, and we get to live here with all the Randells. It's the best life ever."

Nora nodded and kissed him. "That's all I've ever wanted for you."

He grinned. "So be happy." He kissed her cheek, then ran into the cabin.

Brandon came up behind his wife and wrapped his arms around her middle. "You raised a great kid."

She cleared her throat. "Sometimes I think he's the parent."

"He'll always be protective of you. But it's time he's a kid again, and we're all going to make sure of that."

Brandon's family made sure that Zach got to experience true ranch life. They'd all been trained on what diabetic symptoms to look for, and how to handle them.

"It's already working—Zach is thriving." She turned around. "You've had a lot to do with that, Brandon. You've been a good father."

Brandon smiled. "It's easy. All I do is love him." He kissed her. "And love his mother, too."

The door to the cabin opened and Zach rushed out. He gave them both a quick kiss. "Bye, Mom, Dad," he called as he took off up the steps to the parking area about fifty yards away, where Chance waited by his truck.

His uncle waved at them, then cupped his hands and

called. "Come by tomorrow afternoon, and we'll show off Flame's progress."

"Thanks, we might do that," Brandon answered.

With a last wave, Zach and Chance climbed in the truck and drove off.

Brandon untied the horses, and walked them to the lean-to not far from the cabin. The water trough was full and he gave them some grain before he headed back, anticipating a passionate afternoon with his wife.

* * * * *

Harlequin offers a romance for every mood!
See below for a sneak peek from our suspense
romance line
Silhouette® Romantic Suspense.
Introducing HER HERO IN HIDING by
New York Times *bestselling author Rachel Lee.*

Kay Young returned to woozy consciousness to find that she was lying on a soft sofa beneath a heap of quilts near a cheerfully burning fire. When she tried to move, however, everything hurt, and she groaned.

At once she heard a sound, then a stranger with a hard, harsh face was squatting beside her. "Shh," he said softly. "You're safe here. I promise."

"I have to go," she said weakly, struggling against pain. "He'll find me. He can't find me."

"Easy, lady," he said quietly. "You're hurt. No one's going to find you here."

"He will," she said desperately, terror clutching at her insides. "He always finds me!"

"Easy," he said again. "There's a blizzard outside. No one's getting here tonight, not even the doctor. I know, because I tried."

"Doctor? I don't need a doctor! I've got to get away."

"There's nowhere to go tonight," he said levelly. "And if I thought you could stand, I'd take you to a window and show you."

But even as she tried once more to pull away the quilts, she remembered something else: this man had been gentle when he'd found her beside the road, even when she had kicked and clawed. He hadn't hurt her.

Terror receded just a bit. She looked at him and detected signs of true concern there.

The terror eased another notch and she let her head sag on the pillow. "He always finds me," she whispered.

"Not here. Not tonight. That much I can guarantee."

Will Kay's mysterious rescuer protect her
from her worst fears?
Find out in HER HERO IN HIDING by New York
Times *bestselling author Rachel Lee.*
Available June 2010,
only from Silhouette® Romantic Suspense.

HARLEQUIN *Romance*®

GIRLS'
Weekend in
VEGAS

Four friends, four dream weddings!

On a girly weekend in Las Vegas, best friends Alex, Molly,
Serena and Jayne are supposed to just have fun and forget
men, but they end up meeting their perfect matches!
Will the love they find in Vegas stay in Vegas?

Find out in this sassy, fun and wildly romantic miniseries
all about love and friendship!

———————————————

Saving Cinderella! by MYRNA MACKENZIE
Available June

Vegas Pregnancy Surprise by SHIRLEY JUMP
Available July

Inconveniently Wed! by JACKIE BRAUN
Available August

Wedding Date with the Best Man
by MELISSA MCCLONE
Available September

LARGER-PRINT BOOKS!

GET 2 FREE LARGER-PRINT NOVELS PLUS
2 FREE GIFTS!

HARLEQUIN® *Romance*.

From the Heart, For the Heart

YES! Please send me 2 FREE LARGER-PRINT Harlequin® Romance novels and my 2 FREE gifts (gifts are worth about $10). After receiving them, if I don't wish to receive any more books, I can return the shipping statement marked "cancel." If I don't cancel, I will receive 6 brand-new novels every month and be billed just $4.07 per book in the U.S. or $4.47 per book in Canada. That's a saving of at least 22% off the cover price! It's quite a bargain! Shipping and handling is just 50¢ per book.* I understand that accepting the 2 free books and gifts places me under no obligation to buy anything. I can always return a shipment and cancel at any time. Even if I never buy another book from Harlequin, the two free books and gifts are mine to keep forever.

186/386 HDN E5N4

Name _____ (PLEASE PRINT) _____

Address _____ Apt. # _____

City _____ State/Prov. _____ Zip/Postal Code _____

Signature (if under 18, a parent or guardian must sign)

Mail to the **Harlequin Reader Service:**
IN U.S.A.: P.O. Box 1867, Buffalo, NY 14240-1867
IN CANADA: P.O. Box 609, Fort Erie, Ontario L2A 5X3

Not valid for current subscribers to Harlequin Romance Larger-Print books.

Are you a current subscriber to Harlequin Romance books and want to receive the larger-print edition? Call 1-800-873-8635 today!

* Terms and prices subject to change without notice. Prices do not include applicable taxes. N.Y. residents add applicable sales tax. Canadian residents will be charged applicable provincial taxes and GST. Offer not valid in Quebec. This offer is limited to one order per household. All orders subject to approval. Credit or debit balances in a customer's account(s) may be offset by any other outstanding balance owed by or to the customer. Please allow 4 to 6 weeks for delivery. Offer available while quantities last.

Your Privacy: Harlequin Books is committed to protecting your privacy. Our Privacy Policy is available online at www.eHarlequin.com or upon request from the Reader Service. From time to time we make our lists of customers available to reputable third parties who may have a product or service of interest to you. If you would prefer we not share your name and address, please check here. ☐

Help us get it right—We strive for accurate, respectful and relevant communications. To clarify or modify your communication preferences, visit us at www.ReaderService.com/consumerschoice.

HRLP10R

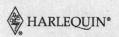 **HARLEQUIN®**

Showcase

Vicki Lewis Thompson

On sale May 11, 2010

Reader favorites from the most talented voices in romance

Save $1.00 on the purchase of 1 or more Harlequin® Showcase books.

SAVE $1.00 on the purchase of 1 or more Harlequin® Showcase books.

Coupon expires Oct 31, 2010. Redeemable at participating retail outlets.
Limit one coupon per purchase. Valid in the U.S.A. and Canada only.

Canadian Retailers: Harlequin Enterprises Limited will pay the face value of this coupon plus 10.25¢ if submitted by customer for this product only. Any other use constitutes fraud. Coupon is nonassignable. Void if taxed, prohibited or restricted by law. Consumer must pay any government taxes. Void if copied. Nielsen Clearing House ("NCH") customers submit coupons and proof of sales to Harlequin Enterprises Limited, P.O. Box 3000, Saint John, NB E2L 4L3, Canada. Non-NCH retailer—for reimbursement submit coupons and proof of sales directly to Harlequin Enterprises Limited, Retail Marketing Department, 225 Duncan Mill Rd., Don Mills, ON M3B 3K9, Canada.

52609015

U.S. Retailers: Harlequin Enterprises Limited will pay the face value of this coupon plus 8¢ if submitted by customer for this product only. Any other use constitutes fraud. Coupon is nonassignable. Void if taxed, prohibited or restricted by law. Consumer must pay any government taxes. Void if copied. For reimbursement submit coupons and proof of sales directly to Harlequin Enterprises Limited, P.O. Box 880478, El Paso, TX 88588-0478, U.S.A. Cash value 1/100 cents.

5 65373 00076 2   (8100)0 11651

HARLEQUIN *Romance*.

Coming Next Month

Available June 8, 2010

#4171 THE LIONHEARTED COWBOY RETURNS
Patricia Thayer
The Texas Brotherhood

#4172 MIRACLE FOR THE GIRL NEXT DOOR
Rebecca Winters
The Brides of Bella Rosa

#4173 THREE TIMES A BRIDESMAID...
Nicola Marsh
In Her Shoes...

#4174 THEIR NEWBORN GIFT
Nikki Logan
Outback Baby Tales

#4175 SAVING CINDERELLA!
Myrna Mackenzie
Girls' Weekend in Vegas

#4176 A DINNER, A DATE, A DESERT SHEIKH
Jackie Braun
Desert Brides